The Crooked Bullet

A Frank Wire Mystery

Rotimi Ogunjobi

Black Rose Writing | Texas

First printing

This is a work of fiction. Names, characters, businesses, places, events, and incidents are either the products of the author's imagination or used in a fictitious manner. Any resemblance to actual persons, living or dead, or actual events is purely coincidental.

ISBN: 978-1-68433-294-6
PUBLISHED BY BLACK ROSE WRITING
www.blackrosewriting.com

Printed in the United States of America
Suggested Retail Price (SRP) $16.95

The Crooked Bullet is printed in Chaparral Pro

To London city with love.
You fixed me and then you broke me again.

The Crooked Bullet

A Frank Wire Mystery

CHAPTER I

Upton Park, London.

Raj Desai sat alone in the back office of his jewelry shop. It was Saturday night, and the staff and security had left; but like every other night, Raj locked up by himself – he was a very careful man.

He opened the front door to peek up and down the street, Bhatti's Jewellery was on Green Street and about a hundred yards away from the tube station. All around, the street this night teemed with African and Asian immigrants, many of whom perpetually looked defeated. Not a lot different from what he and his wife must have looked like when they had come to live here more than two decades ago, he knew. The only appreciable commercial traffic at this time was from the Tesco supermarket. It wasn't football day, else the pubs around would have been rowdy with drunken revellers from the stadium down the road where Westham FC played their home matches. Here on these streets, spotted with phlegm and perpetually smelling of disinfectant, he and his late wife had nevertheless found good fortune

Raj shut the door and turned the key. He failed, however, to see Kalyan Shetty his son-in-law to be, running down from the train station. Kalyan knocked eagerly on the door just as Raj turned away. He is dressed in a dark suit; obviously coming from work. Raj again opened the door to let him in and then drew down the electric operated front window security grille.

"Good evening Papa. How are you today?" Kalyan asked.

"Very well thank you, my son. You are coming from work?" Raj Desai replied. They both spoke in Hindi,

"Yes Papa. Rupinder says to meet her at home, but it is too early since she does not arrive from work at the hospital for another two hours. So I thought to come have a chat with you, and then maybe go home along with you," Kalyan said.

"That is fine. She works long hours at the hospital sometimes. Too long for a woman even if a doctor." Raj regretted.

They both entered Raj's office at the back of the shop floor. Conspicuous on a wall of the cramped office were three portraits. One was of his deceased wife Sangita, her scowl still intimidating even in the picture. The second was of his only daughter Rupinder in her graduation attire from medical school. The third portrait was of Raj, Sangita and Rupinder, taken twenty-two years back in Mumbai, and when Rupinder was just about three years old.

Raj looked up and pointed to the picture of Rupinder.

"She takes after her mother. Unfortunately, Sangita died when Rupinder was still a little child and left us alone." he seemed to apologise.

"I am always sorry to hear that Papa. You have done quite well, however." Kalyan told him.

"Oh no, she has done quite well. All that you see here in this shop means nothing to me. This shop, Bhatti's Jewellery belonged to Sangita, and she made it a success by hard work. Only she taught me enough to be able to make it prosper still. This shop we bought the shop from her uncle, Shami "Bhatti" Bhatnagar. He was widowed, quite fed up with his bad arthritis and going back home to New Delhi. We came here poor, she determined to make us rich, and rich we became. Bhatti's belongs to Sangita, my son, Rupinder is my only success. You will take care of Rupinder for me when you eventually get married will you?" Raj asked

"I promise Papa; I promise." Kalyan patted his hand.

Raj opened a solid wood locker and brought out a black box, expensively decorated with black velvet and gold trimmings and about the size of a medium-size pizza box. Inside, the box was lined with purple satin. It contained a gold pendant attached to a gold chain. The pendant has the shape of a bent bullet.

"Look at this; what do you think?" Raj eagerly asked.

"It is beautiful Papa, and it looks very valuable," Kalyan confessed.

"Yes it is valuable. It is the Crooked Bullet. It is supposed to bring peace to the marriage. By family tradition, it must be passed to the first son to get married in the family as it had been passed down for five generations. But since I do not have a son, I will give it to you."

"Thank you, Papa. I will take care of it and cherish it.," Kalyan was pleased to learn.

"The pendant must not be lost though, else the result will be a life plagued with great hardship for many generations following." Raj Desai warned.

"It will not be lost, Papa. I promise to keep it and also give it to your grandson when the time comes." Kalyan promised

Raj closed the box, quite lovingly tucked it away again in the locker and turned the key. Then he opened a big steel safe door to put the key in. The safe contained a lot of money which had been carelessly thrown in. He changed his mind; opened the locker once again, took out the box and put it in the safe, nodding his head in satisfaction that this made more sense.

"You have too much money in that safe Papa; you ought to take it to the bank at the end of every day." Kalyan worried.

"Yes I know. There must be more than a hundred thousand pounds inside there, which are the cash sales for the entire day. Too many customers prefer to pay cash for jewellery you know. Sangita would have insisted that the cash should be taken to the night deposit at the bank down the road, but never mind I will do that in the morning. Nobody is coming to steal a safe my son, this is London." Raj reasoned. Up on the wall, the scowling picture of Sangita seemed to accuse him even more and to make him momentarily nervous.

"After you and Rupinder are married, I think I will sell the shop and like old man Shami "Bhatti" Bhatnagar, return home to Mumbai." He declared

They both exit the office, switching off the lights behind them. Raj engaged the shop security system, after which they both exit the shop through a side door, which Raj also locked. Raj's car, a Mercedes, was parked a few yards away, and both walked slowly toward it.

There was still a bit of a chill outside; summer was still several weeks away. Raj pushed his wool cap tighter on his head and wrapped his coat tighter around him. He had been thinking of what to do next. When you were nearly sixty, life seemed to become so routine, and the choices available for nearly everything became so few. Before Kalyan arrived, he had been trying to make a choice between having dinner at the Hyderabad Darbar Restaurant down the road or going nearer home at Romford to Aroma on High Street. And maybe thereafter going to The Bitter End pub for a pint or two and a chat with the denizens. Now he wasn't quite sure anymore what to do with himself, his coveted companionship with loneliness suddenly broken

"Give me the key Papa, I will drive you home," Kalyan suggested. They both entered the car and drove away into the darkness.

● ● ● ● ●

Later that night, a grim conference took place at an upmarket health spa known as Woodstock. The place, located near Chigwell had previously been a farm. Now it was a celebrity hideout – where the annual membership was rumored to cost nearly as much as a brand new Rolls Royce. The rules inside Woodstock were for those to whom money meant very little – primary of those rules being that shoes were not permitted to be worn within the grounds of the estate.

The office in which the night conference took place looked quite like it had been time-warped from the sixties. Moses Samuel or Rabbi Zulu as the proprietor of Woodstock was more fondly called, was having a discussion with four men of Eastern Europe stock. Also in his office were three other people, one of them his closest aide Sasha Cohen, a slightly plump lady who habitually wore dark John Lennon glasses.

The huge room was completely decorated with vintage furniture and fittings; including a large Beatles grandfather clock and an RCA radiogram. On one of the walls were two huge posters each of them about eight feet tall. One was of the singer Isaac Hayes playing at the Sahara Tahoe in the "70s – with dark aviator sunglasses, a heavy chain around his neck, naked to the waist and looking so sweaty sexy. It was an image Moses Samuel always faithfully tried to imitate to the limit that his own white skin would permit. The other poster was of a barefooted Masai warrior in full battle leap. This was the one around which he had built the new philosophies behind his life and business.

Only one of the four men in attendance spoke English, but they all nevertheless understood the instructions that were being passed to them.

"The bank is in Hackney. It was in there that a person I knew, hard-working man, lost his home to them way back and killed himself as a consequence, do you understand?"

The men nodded.

"Yah, yah"; they understood. They also still understood the intolerable iniquities of uncontrolled capitalist economics.

Moses Samuel pointed to a television camera on the table before them.

"See this thing? Real techie stuff. I had it specially made for me in China. It is not only a camera; it will also scramble all CCTV signals and disable all other security equipment, and so nobody will be able to understand what happened. After the job, you will drive away to Dover from where you will cross the channel and then get a plane to Brazil. By the time you return home in a couple of months, you will have no worries. Plus you will be rich."

Sasha gave the leader of the men a large envelope which contained plane tickets, some fake travel documents. They nodded quietly and left with the television camera.

Moses Samuel switched on the huge gleaming imitation vintage RCA radiogram standing in a corner of the room, and eagerly twiddled the tuning dial till he found the channel he was looking for. It was a rogue radio channel. A hip-hop remix of an Earth Wind and Fire ballad seeped out of the large speakers of the retro-modern music center.

You will find peace of mind
If you look way down in your heart and soul
Don't hesitate "cause the world seems cold
Stay young at heart "cause you're never (never, never...) old at heart

"He's good, isn't he?" Moses Samuel nodded his head, and at the same time seeking the ladies' approval.

"Yes, He's cool," Sasha said. The other girl in the room was not so committal; neither was the small, bespectacled young man who looked like a newspaper guy. They didn't understand this type of music.

"I'd surely enjoy working with this guy. We do have a lot in common," Moses Samuel said.

"Half of London is dying to know who he is. Keeps extremely modest for a musician, I think. I admire that," said Sasha.

"Ex-Man," Moses Samuel gushed. "Ex-Man; the most mysterious and perhaps the most talented musician in England. I love the name - Superhero; superstar."

"I've got to go to bed now Rabbi," Sasha said with a reverent bow. Moses Samuel pleasantly waved both ladies goodbye.

"This job you asked those men to do at the bank, do you think it has a hope of success?" the young man asked.

"Why not?" Moses Samuel seemed surprised that anyone could think this way.

"Oh well; robbing a bank with a camera. It seems such a ridiculous notion as I see it," the man truthfully opined.

"Exactly," Moses Samuel agreed with him. "And it is because it looks so ridiculous that is why it will succeed. Difficult to rob a bank with a machine gun; a hundred times easier to rob a bank with a camera."

Together they had a good laugh over their ridiculous plan. The young man shut his laptop computer and lugged it out of the room, with a reverent bow at the door.

Alone in the office, at last, Moses Samuel sat behind his huge ornate oak desk nodding and humming to the music. Ex-Man's weekly hour-long broadcast had become a phenomenon - regularly bringing the boredom index in London crashing down every Sunday night. The pirate radio came on around eleven till midnight and then completely disappeared from the air till the next week. Within a short time, it had become one hour that discerning Londoner came to look forward to.

Much of Ex-Man's music was not new. Much of it was really a remix of old tunes but done in ways that nobody had ever thought possible. Now, Moses Samuel thought, here was one musician worth putting money on to go places. Ex-Man's first single - "*Dynomite*," had just about a month ago, hit the chart and quickly climbed up as fast as a monkey with its tail on fire. But still, nobody knew who Ex-Man was and so deliciously, neither was he going about advertising his identity.

Dynomite had been quietly released by Def *Adam* - a new and unknown private label - no parties, no press. *Def Adam* as he found out was owned by an Isle of Man company of the same name but with nominee directors, and the distribution of the four records of the label so far was being done by Michael Jah, a Jamaican agent from a shop hemmed in between two vegetable shops right inside Brixton Market. There the trail had gone dead.

"I just sell records man, I don't sell comics. Yeah man," the seemingly perplexed records broker had reasoned with him.

Moses Samuel had subsequently been even more intrigued by and full of respect for this unknown artist. Certainly not like any of the no-talent wannabes parading selves as musicians on the strength of being able to ingest a lot of mind-bending chemicals and scream at the top of their voices as a consequence; the papers were always plastered with their stupid faces.

Who was Ex-man? Ironically, that mystery really had contributed in a major way to the success of the new record. Moses Samuel loved that bit of irony. As a matter of fact, it was the same sort of device which had moved his life and business forward.

He walked over to another table on which sat the one-foot high scale model of what was a shopping mall, though anyone else could have called it an art gallery. It was two-stories high, looked about a hundred yards wide and was painted up like Andy Warhol had been at work on it. *Who is Moses Samuel?* Yes, they did have a lot in common, him and Ex-Man; they were both definitely destined to go places. Probably together.

CHAPTER 2

Dynoooomite!!

The wide-mouthed black youth looked like J.J. Walker from the old time TV series Good Times. He was wearing a hooded sweatshirt and doing a mime to Ex-Man's remix of Tony Camillo's *Dynomite* on MTV. Frank O'Dwyer woke up to find the time was ten o'clock. He was horrified. When you had a boss who didn't like you very much, and you woke up at ten o" clock on Monday morning, you knew dead cert that your ass was already grass.

Frank had fallen asleep on the couch, as he realized. An open can of Guinness was spilled on the carpet. He had no recollection of when he had popped the can or switched on the TV; he also couldn't tell for certain how he had got home last night. It had been really a hell of a gig and a demon or two were still trapped in his head, hacking away with sharp axes and picks. Frank picked up his mobile phone and called his office at East End Mirror.

"Ellen, I am going to be a bit late this morning, I am not feeling so well," he told Ellen Wescott, the secretary.

"Frank, you had a meeting scheduled for nine thirty with Spencer, and He's hopping mad. Better come in as soon as you can, but I think you're dead meat already," Ellen told him.

Frank's heart sank. It was the day of the monthly departmental meeting with his boss Spencer Cowley *aka The Beast;* who also owned the East End Mirror newspaper. As the journalist who handled the crime beat, Frank's absence wouldn't go unnoticed, at least not by Spencer who seemed quite lately to have a special place in his heart for him - a place where poisons were kept.

David Fernandez would be there of course. David was the bespectacled young Indian rookie journalist who presently covered the trivia departments and the cocktail circuit. David was okay really - quite friendly and efficient. He was also very unnaturally gifted with computers, and so prodigiously prolific that Frank suspected the little guy had programmed his computer to crank out fake stories.

David did remind him of a longtime foe Phil Jenner, who used to work with The Independent but had somehow just disappeared; like fallen off the face of the earth. Phil Jenner had been quite a terror to Frank's life because Spencer Cowley always compared Frank's puny effort to the prodigious Phil Jenner. And so prolific had Phil Jenner been that it appeared he manufactured his own stories – like when he wanted to report a murder, he just went off and killed somebody. But somehow he disappeared, and life had since then become more bearable for Frank – until David Fernandez showed up. Later though, Frank had learned to his shame that David Fernandez just made more creative use of Google and Yahoo! Frank had afterward learned to live amicably with David since their tasks rarely encroached.

Somewhere along the line though, Spencer had determined that newspapers thrived more on gossip and trivia than on real news and thus had David become to be much more seriously reckoned with at the East End Mirror. And as David grew in importance so had Frank begun to feel his own relevance diminished. In his nightmares, the little Indian guy now played a significantly menacing role, and as a matter of fact, Frank suspected that David was being prepared to take over from him in the event of his demise, which now seemed quite near.

Never one to distress nevertheless, Frank took off his seven-inch wide plaque which said MC Wire, had a quick shower, coffee, a burnt buttered toast, and eventually set out for work. Trevor *"The Mad Scientist"* Cook, his tandem deejay act, did bring him home last night, he knew. Trevor had just bought a new BMW, and they'd together taken it for a spin to Brighton for a gig along with two mad West Indian chicks and two cases of wine. Pity he couldn't now remember the girls' names.

The sun seemed unusually bright and hot this morning; shining with such intense malice. The entire world seemed to jog along sluggishly around him like gargantuan mobile Dali sculptures. Frank's flat was mere minutes from Hackney Central, which was not too crowded at this time. From there he caught a bus to the office of the East End Mirror, located in Shoreditch, ten minutes away.

It was an open-plan office containing ten cubicles on either side of a central aisle. A conference room, as well as the office of the proprietor Spencer Cowley, was at the far end. Frank slipped in quietly, said a quick hello to Fernandez with whom he shared a cubicle. Frank had barely sat down at his desk when Spencer Cowley breezed by. He is a burly man with fat jowls and a booming voice

"Could you come with me for a little chat Frank," he said, without a pause in his steps and without looking in his direction. Frank noted that nobody was looking in his direction either. The greetings this morning had been quite lukewarm all around - something heavy definitely seemed expected.

Frank found Spencer in the small conference room at the end of the corridor which ran the entire length of the office. Everyone remembered the room as the place where major negotiations were made: such as hiring, promotion, ass-kicking, and firing. Spencer was smoking a cigar when Frank came in, and Frank felt an irresponsible urge to point to the No Smoking sign on the wall. An irresponsible urge because here at the East End Mirror, Spencer Cowley, owner, Chief Executive, and Chief Editor was the law.

"Good morning Spencer. Sorry I was late. I wasn't feeling well this morning when I woke up," Frank apologised.

"Oh, of course, yes, and I guess I am the cause of it, isn't that right? Especially as this happens so frequently. Frank, what do you think this place is about?" Spencer didn't sound amused.

Frank grimaced. He had a very bad headache which was presently being exacerbated by Spencer's loud voice. He looked away into the clear glass tabletop and doodled nervously on it with a finger.

"Frank, do you honestly think this newspaper is a joke?" Spencer asked, puffing violently on his cigar like a mad marijuana fiend. Frank thought this a trick question and safely kept quiet. Besides, his head hurt like hell.

"Let me put it another way, Frank, do you honestly enjoy working here?"

Against common sense, Frank this time around had an irresponsible impression that Spencer genuinely had his best interest at heart; like your anxious mother hassling you for spending the whole night out at a party. Frank looked away into the clear glass table and doodled nervously on the top with a finger.

"No I don't enjoy working here, Spencer," he truthfully replied; and this did somehow make him feel good.

"So why don't you be man enough about it then and quit?" Spencer said to him, and this made Frank feel bad.

"I'm sorry I didn't mean to say that" Frank apologized. Too late though; he found Spencer looking into his eyes with contrived pity, slowly and very sadly shaking his head.

"I'm sorry I've got to let you go Frank," Spencer said to him; and this made Frank feel a lot worse. He tried to feel man enough about it nevertheless.

"Don't I get any kind of notice?"

"Your contract entitles you to one month notice Frank, but never mind. I have signed you a check for the next month, and you can leave today," Spencer told him, offering a sweaty handshake. "If you need references, I will be pleased to give you some. I've already given Ellen a check for you, and you may collect it immediately. Good luck Frank."

Frank returned to his desk and silently began to empty the drawers. The entire office seemed unusually quiet and busy around him. He felt angry with them all, with Spencer Cowley and most of all with himself for handing Spencer the perfect excuse to throw him out, right on a golden platter. It hadn't been a great job, but it paid the bills. Ellen came around a few minutes later with his check.

"He's in a hellish mood today, innit?" She commiserated.

"Yeah, well it's got to happen one day; and I guess the sooner, the better," Frank puts up his brave front.

Fernandez came over, cautiously.

"What happened over there Frank?" he worriedly asked.

"Just lost my job. I guess you will be doing the crime watch circuit all by yourself for a while, unless Spencer has found a replacement for me yet." Frank wheezed.

"That's awful. What are you going to do now Frank?" Fernandez sounded genuinely concerned.

"I don't know yet. You never plan to lose your job, I believe, or do you? I'll get by somehow, I am sure." Frank shrugged his shoulders.

"I'm happy you can think like that. It's all really no more than just a job, see? Just hang on to that truth and you won't feel so bad anymore," Ellen advised.

"Thanks Ellen," Frank said to her and signed the voucher for his check.

"Good luck Frank, we're going to miss you." Ellen shook his hand

"Going to really miss you, Bro. I know we didn't get along so well on some issues, but I really think you are a great guy. Namaste." Fernandez also emotionally took his hand.

Frank emptied much of the contents of his desk into the bin. They were mostly half-written stories which were long dead. This completed, he left the office of East End Mirror, giving one last tired salute at the door, and his few prized possessions in a little box under his arm. Spencer Cowley standing menacingly in the middle of the news office returned the salute.

Frank caught a bus home from Shoreditch to Hackney Central, looking pensively out of the window all through the journey. At Hackney Central, he bought some fruits from a stall and walked to his flat which was about two hundred yards away.

It was still just around midday. He found it strange and a really confusing experience to be home at this time of the day.

Frank put the fruits in the fridge, took out a can of Guinness and lay on the sofa to watch MTV. The Ex-Man's newly released video was still getting prime time play treatment. Every time he heard the song, he always got this feeling that he knew the voice even though it had been passed through a synthesizer. But then a lot of rap often sounded quite like the same, unless you were doing it in some patent way like Snoop Dogg or even like Grandmaster Flash, who he very much thought was the boss. Frank soon drifted off to sleep.

There were three missed calls on his phone when he woke up. He dialed his voice mail. There was one message from Trevor:

"How are you doing, Frankie? You did have quite a skinfull last night, didn't you? Talk later" [click]. The second message brought him fully awake.

"Hi Frankie, it's me Nancy. You'll call me back, will you? [Click]." No, he wouldn't. Nancy Hughes was an old flame, who had *house stepped* on her foot three weeks ago at a rave party. Life had a way of working funny new habits into lonely people's lives because as much as Frank had ever known, Nancy was chronically agoraphobic and would rather watch a golf game on television than from the middle of a mile wide green. That was how shocked he had been to find Nancy at a rave, where six dozen lunatics were getting smashed on cheap booze and screaming above the deafening music.

The third was from his mum in Manchester, wanting to make sure that he was still wearing clothes and not walking around naked in the night like all those hooligans. Now, Frank knew this was an important message, and if he didn't reply to his mum's call, she would probably come knocking on his door the next morning. So Frank called mum and assured her yes, he still was wearing clothes; no he wasn't wearing manacles around his neck; no he wasn't smoking pot yet, and yes, he's still got a job - the last one being now a lie.

He returned to watching television. Again the video of an EX-MAN rap rendition of Herbie Hancock's "Chameleon" was playing on MTV. He liked it.

CHAPTER 3

When Frank woke up the next morning, he found three more missed calls on his phone. They were all from the same number and certainly didn't belong to anyone in his phone directory. Frank had a policy of not returning missed calls from unknown callers – primarily because it costs money and again you never know whom they are from. From experience, unknown callers usually spelled trouble – debt collectors, tax office, and bank calling about your un-approved overdraft.

It was a nice Tuesday morning, and Frank was just getting into the routine of preparing for work until it suddenly occurred to him that hey you got no job, man. Nevertheless, he dressed up. The unemployed always have a place to go - the Jobcentre never turned anyone away. And in any case, the Jobcentre was the logical place to start looking for another job – theoretically.

He took Spencer Cowley's check with him, tucking it into his shirt's pocket; and thinking to visit the bank, later in the day. The check was not for a lot, and he didn't imagine it would take him quite far. So he definitely needed to get a job really fast, primarily because the rent needed to get paid by the first day of each month, which was just about a week away. The last thing he needed at this time was to have himself thrown in the street. Frank thought the check was mischief really because he usually got paid by bank transfer. It occurred to him that Spencer intended to make a statement with the check - like he didn't want to have anything more to do with Frank.

Hey, here is your pay you fucker; now get the hell out of here and don't ever come back.

Frank hated visiting the Jobcentre, primarily because as everyone knew, it was the place where you went in hopeful and came out hopeless. There, as he expected, he found himself in the company of the drunk, the druggies, and the born layabouts—all waiting to be fed into the omnivorous mill of the unemployment benefit processing machine.

He made a quick start at the job search computer, and it confirmed because that seemed its only purpose for which it seemed to have been made, that there was no job available for journalists within 50 miles of Hackney. Not about to completely lose hope though, Frank joined the queue to see an employment officer.

"What kind of job are you looking for?" the lady asked. Frank had a feeling that she didn't care, and was just going through the rote.

"I am a journalist," Frank told her. She tapped some keys on her computer, and ruefully shook her head.

"No journalist job here," she said.

"I know that; I just checked from the computer by myself and couldn't find any listing. I thought maybe you had some other jobs that haven't been yet listed." Frank replied, mildly annoyed.

"Would you be willing to consider any other job?"

Frank had a fleeting thought that having a full-time job as a disc jockey would have been so cool but he didn't think they made jobs in that model yet; at least not in London.

"Yes, depending on what you have available. I really must pay my bills somehow," Frank replied. Humming gaily, she tapped some more on her computer.

"I have got some vacancies for truck drivers. Do you have a license?"

"No I don't have a license to drive anything on wheels," Frank laughed; thinking he had no desire to drive a fucking truck.

"Door security?" She again suggested.

"I have a problem standing for long," Frank told her.

"You wouldn't consider a street cleaning job either I guess because of your disability?" Frank imagined she was mocking him, with the way she said, "your disability." Nevertheless, he just shook his head, thinking no way was he going to be scooping dog poop for anybody.

"Traffic warden?" She asked. Again Frank laughed and shook his head. As far as he knew, nearly everyone who owned a car was looking for a traffic warden to murder.

"Okay then, could you check back next week and we might hopefully have something along your street. In the interim would you like to sign on to receive unemployment benefits?"

At this time a mail boy passed – probably sixteen years old or so.

Get off that chair and go do some work like a man you lazy motherfucker; his disgusted eyes seemed to say to Frank.

"No I don't want to sign on for anything," Frank told her.

"Suit yourself then," she said.

Frank's bank was only a hundred yard down the street, and it took him less than five minutes to get there. A small bus with BBC stencilled on the sides was parked outside the bank, but he didn't really pay attention to that.

The bank was a little crowded which didn't make sense, not so early in the morning.

"What's going on?" he'd asked the door security.

"A little bit of equipment malfunction, but I am sure all will be back to normal in a few minutes. We were alerted," the tall happy Nigerian told him. Frank seated himself near an old West Indian granny while he waited for the queue to get moving once more.

"Hello my dearie, I am Mrs. Williams.," the granny told him. Frank shook her hand and told her his own name.

"My name is Frank. I learn the computers have gone funny, that's odd, isn't it?" he asked.

"Nothing odd at all dearie; the bank is full of funny business these days, aren't they? Last year me bring me check here. You know we old citizens get some allowance for our heating equipment and stuff. Now me hand me check over to one of this *rass* teller over there you see, and next time I look back he gone. Went away with my money; an old woman money. And so about an hour later he back again, and me kick a fuss and lick him on the head with me bag. Give me back me money you thief me shout at him. And his supervisor come and beg me cool *doun*; cool *doun* he say because all the man do is go for break. Cool *doun, bloodclat* say to me. Can you believe that, young man? Idiot boy go for break with me money."

Frank nodded miserably and agreed with Mrs. Williams that yes, all bank workers were thieves and must be put in prison. But she was not even halfway done yet. Mrs. Williams proceeded to recite her biography and especially the rather touching bit about her granddaughter Harriet, whose picture she carried around in her handbag and was pleased to show Frank.

"You know Harriet, poor girl who shouldn't have married the goat goes by the name of Winston who can't keep a job and all he do is play trumpet in a reggae band as if he in Jamaica. This is sad because living in London is hard man; not like back-a-yard in Jamaica."

It made Frank guilty that this nice lonely lady Mrs. Williams actually thought she was talking to a nice young white man who had his life altogether. Nevertheless, he obediently nodded and agreed to all she said.

In an open cubicle a dejected Antipodean was trying to convince his personal banker that he qualified for an overdraft, but from the look on his face, he was not making any progress at all. The banker punched some keys on her computer, made some busy humming noise, and came to a final verdict or more correctly the computer came to a final verdict. She shook her head.

But Ozzie was not giving up easily His life depended on getting the overdraft, this being perfectly understandable since he had just lost his job, was living in a rented house with a pregnant wife, and his immigration status did not qualify him for unemployment benefit.

"For three years I have faithfully made this particular bank home to my salary, and if not for this unfortunate incident I wouldn't need an overdraft," he desperately pleaded his case; but the bank computer remained merciless.

Frank eventually had a chance to cash his check. He thought he should have just paid the check into his account, but another thought came to him to cash the check first.

In another part of the bank, a camera crew of four from BBC had been interviewing the bank supervisor, who was happily enjoying the show and describing how the bank security system worked. The camera crew from BBC was now leaving the bank. They were leaving with a box which looked full of money – and yes it was. The supervisor grinned at the camera, enjoying the show and explaining how the security system captured this sort of situation. Out went the camera crew into a van that had pulled up in front of the bank. The supervisor waved them away. The agreement appeared to have been for the van to drive round the block for five minutes or so and come back with the box of money, and then for the camera crew to see in the bank's security office how the whole event had been faithfully recorded.

"Hey your bank has been robbed," Frank told the supervisor who patiently paced the banking hall, waiting for the camera crew from BBC that failed to return.

"Of course not, they are from BBC," he scolded – through a mind which was clogging up with fear.

"But you have been robbed, those blokes left with your money."

"I know sir, but they will be back in a minute. They are doing a documentary on bank security for BBC."

"I'll be fucked if they come back," Frank told him.

Now very sweaty the supervisor disappeared into his office. A couple of minutes later, two police squad cars wailed to a stop in front of the bank and three officers hasted toward the supervisor's office.

"The bank has been robbed," Frank told Mrs. Williams.

"Really? Praise the lord, serve them right for a change," Mrs. Williams was joyful. Struck with joy, the Australian loan-seeker, proudly stood from his chair in front of the personal banker and her *evil* computer; his face ecstatic.

"The bank has been robbed," Ozzie joyfully muttered over and over as he left the bank. Finally outside he couldn't contain his happiness anymore. He went leaping like he had experienced a profound miracle. And off he went, broadcasting the triumph of justice over greed straight into the path of a speeding Bus 242. And even as he breathed his last, a rapturous expression rested on his face.

"The fucking bank has been robbed," he silently shouted.

"Who said that?" asked the supervisor who again returned to the banking hall this time in the company of the three unsmiling police.

"I did" Frank volunteered.

"Can you step this way for a minute please," one of the policemen beckoned with his head. Frank found himself hustled into the supervisor's office.

"How much do you know about this?" he was asked "Nothing more than I saw with my eyes while standing to cash my check," Frank told them.

"You don't know any of those men from BBC?"

"Of course not; any fool could have seen that heist coming" Frank chuckled.

The supervisor glared; he clearly didn't like being called any fool. But in any case, he knew that in a matter of hours he was likely to be without a job and quite likely to be in need of a lawyer to save his behind from prison. His wife and children were going to be angry with him for a long time. They finally let Frank go after taking his identification.

Outside Frank found the building cordoned off behind police tape. The bank was now a crime scene. A large crowd had gathered to learn what had happened. Mrs. William was there right before them all; basking in the spotlight as a witness to the crime. A smaller and now dispersing crowd had gathered to see the remains of Ozzie being taken away by an ambulance.

•   •   •   •   •

Frank usually went to the Hard Luck Café on Lower Clapton Road to catch up on the latest news and stuff. Usually never before sundown, but today he needed somewhere to go, was short of ideas, so he ended up at the Hard Luck Café for an early lunch.

"What is the matter Frank, you're not at work?" Lester Bowie asked. Lester was the waiter at the Hard Luck Café – once a temporary draft from the Dinosaurs Over-50s Employment Network. Lester always kept the customers irritated or amused but never alone, so Maureen Smith the owner of the café had retained him now for more than two years. At fifty-two Lester still didn't really know what his life was about and appeared not to care anymore.

"None of your businesses, Frank told him.

"Well, since when have you ever come into here at quarter past noon to order Bubble and Squeak and a Guinness? So I say what *ales* you." Lester chuckled, putting a pun on the "ale."

"Fuck off and do your job Lester," Frank told him.

He had picked up a copy of the Sun at a newsstand near Hackney Central, and he dived lustfully into the page three half taken up by a topless model.

"Nekkid girl, what she selling den," Maureen laughed behind him.

"Hi Maureen," Frank flashed her smile. Maureen was the owner of Hard Luck Cafe, forty-something full-breasted beauty with a motherly smile. Maureen always minded her business and didn't hassle you with questions. Lester came back with Frank's food at last and set it on the table with a wink.

"Dirty newspaper pictures make you go blind you know?" he said.

"Fuck off," Frank waved him away, and silently ate his food while reading the paper.

Become a Private Investigator.

Somewhere in the last pages of the paper Frank again saw a small advertisement that he had noticed the previous day. It was about a private detective course or something like that. There was a phone number at the bottom of the advertisement, and having nothing else to do after his meal, he called the number.

The call was taken by a giggly girl who answered, "Hi my name is Mandy, and how may I help you?" .Frank extracted the address of Eagle Detective Training Institute from Mandy. It was somewhere near Elephant and Castle, and since it was the right day for time wasting, Frank thought why not check it out.

While making the call to Eagle Detective Institute, Frank found that he had a missed call, and so he called his voicemail. Nancy had left another message.

Nancy. He hadn't seen her in years and wondered what it was she wanted. Frank and Nancy had together kept a single bedroom apartment together for almost a year. It had been so wonderful initially, two kids just having fun in all possible ways. Then Nancy had started to want more, hinting at marriage. For a guy without a steady job getting hitched wasn't a thought that Frank thought he wanted to mess with, so he had persistently navigated away off the topic as well as he could.

But Nancy had also remained persistent, and it soon became that the only way to avoid talking about getting married was to avoid speaking with Nancy and eventually to avoid seeing Nancy, which was pretty difficult, for two people living together in a single bedroom flat.

Then Thomas had appeared on the scene. Frank had initially become sure that Nancy was seeing someone else. How else to explain that some weirdo kept sending in flowers every day

"Hey, what's with all these flowers; the flat's like a fucking undertaker's," Frank complained to Nancy.

"None of your business," she had tersely replied; which was partly correct because even though they shared the rent, the lease of the flat was in her name. And even though Frank was relieved that Nancy was no more discussing marriage, the flowers still kept him freaked; like they forebode someone's funeral.

Frank came in one night to hear moaning noises from the room which he used to share with Nancy before the living room couch became more comfortable for him. The bedroom door was open, and on the bed, he found Nancy with one of his friends, Thomas Pawney; both them naked. Angry from both the effrontery and the betrayals, Frank hauled Thomas naked out of the flat. Nancy had also done the expected and thrown Frank's stuff out of her flat that very night.

Looking back, Frank thought that was the best thing that happened to him and Nancy. He remembered sleeping on the buses that night. Well, there wasn't really much sleep. He just got himself on whichever bus was going the furthest distance and tried to get some sleep during the journeys. And at the terminus, he changed into another going the other way and got a bit more sleep on the way. That was how that night had passed.

Jay Winch had been a lucky find the next day. Jay, a software guy, was going off to do some better paying gig in Chicago or wherever and needed someone to mind his flat for a couple of years. So with no reference and without a deposit, Frank had quite impossibly found himself the proud tenant of a two bedroom flat in Hackney. Next day he called Nancy and quite maliciously told her how much he wished her and Thomas Pawney a miserable lifetime and a house full of retarded children together.

But somehow and quite impossibly Nancy Hughes had shown up at a rave party at Dalston a few weeks back, without her Thomas Pawney. Nancy had come along with two plump Scottish girls on a suicide mission from Glasgow, and who had spent the entire night knocking down Vodka shots, and the rest of the early morning vomiting them up on the sidewalk.

"What happened to Thomas Pawney?" Frank found a minute to ask Nancy during the night.

"Not my type, he wanted to marry me," Nancy told Frank; leaving him with the conviction that most women are mad?

"Thought that was what you wanted," Frank reminded her.

"Yes with you maybe; not with Thomas Pawney. I don't love him," she ruefully smiled. Being afraid of what was coming up Frank took off but not quickly enough to prevent Nancy from getting his phone number. He now ruefully regretted he had not given her a wrong number. And so, there on my phone was Nancy for the umpteenth time in a month asking him to return her call.

Lester was watching the television with Maureen since no other customer was yet about. They were watching a football match between Liverpool FC and Arsenal. Lester normally looked to Frank a hopeless case in his plaid apron, but today Lester really did strike him differently, and invoked respect. At least Lester had a job going for him.

"You done guv?" Lester asked. Frank gave him the OK sign, took out money from his wallet and bailed himself from the Hard Luck Cafe.

CHAPTER 4

Frank found Eagle Detective Training Institute on the second floor of the mall at Elephant and Castle. It was a sparsely furnished small office, with only one desk, behind which he found Mandy seated, quite engrossed with her OK magazine. An ornately framed black and white portrait of a distinguished looking gentleman with handlebar mustache supervised his discussion with the giggly Mandy, who was the o.

"I called you about one hour ago about the detective course," Frank explained to her.

"Yes, you did. It is, of course, a home study course, and it normally costs four hundred pounds, but you can buy for only two hundred and forty-nine pounds and ninety-nine pence at the discount price if you buy today.," Mandy went straight to business.

"That's a lot of money, is there an installment payment option?" Frank asked.

"No, unfortunately. It's a bargain though, and there is a certificate inside the package. After you are done with your studying you just print your name on the certificate put it in a frame and hang it in your office to prove that you are a real detective," Mandy actually failed to see how ridiculous she sounded. She went into a store behind the office, came out with a box which she placed on the table in front of Frank.

"Heck, I can't read all this," Frank told her. Mandy shrugged her shoulder.

"In any case for ninety-nine pounds extra you could purchase the entire courses recorded on CDs and listen to be trained as a detective," she advised.

"That sounds better. Okay, I will just have the CDs then." Frank happily offered. Mandy firmly shook her head.

"No, the CDs must be bought together with the books, not alone. Don't be lazy with your studies; it is not easy to become a detective you know." she playfully scolded.

"That's a lot of money," Frank scratched his head thoughtfully.

"Well, the advertisement did say that you could actually earn a hundred quid per hour as a private detective so this is cheap. You get all your money back in four hours." Mandy shrugged and giggled some more.

The man in the portrait appeared to glare at him with much disapproval. Frank handed his bank card to Mandy for payment. Mandy was glad to pass Frank's card through a processing machine which dutifully deducted three hundred and forty pounds from his bank account. Mandy cheerfully wrote him a receipt.

"Who is the bloke in the picture? Is that the owner of this business? Out of curiosity, he pointed to the portrait.

"I don't know; I met him here," Mandy replied, returning to reading her OK Magazine.

Frank left Eagle Detective Training. He checked his phone again and found that he had another missed call. He called his voicemail; Nancy had left another message. Frank grimaced.

●　　　●　　　●　　　●　　　●

Lugging the parcel home took all the energy out of him. Nevertheless, back at home, he ripped open the seal of one of the boxes. He popped one of the CDs into a portable player. It was topic number two of the detective course and the title from the cover said: Tracing Missing Persons. Frank thought this could be the most interesting part of the entire course. He grimaced at the badly recorded voice of the instructor, who had obviously been reading from the course notes. He sat on the couch to listen nonetheless and was soon lulled to sleep.

When he woke up, it was around six o'clock in the evening. Taking a quick shower, he decided to visit his girlfriend. He took a bus for Stratford Station, and at the station, exit bought a bunch of flowers and walked up to a nearby block of flats. He took the lift to the second floor and pressed the bell at the second door to the right of the lift, which was where Sade Leigh lived Hers was a two-room job, a room of which she had converted into a garment design studio. Sade was a vivacious Nigerian dressmaker, with a very colorful taste, in clothes. Frank would often wonder what she admired in him since they seemed exactly opposite in almost every way.

•　　•　　•　　•　.　•

"Vegetables again," Sade groaned, taking the bouquet Frank had brought and putting it in a vase.

"They aren't vegetables honey, they are the best. They cost me a bunch at the station." Frank laughed.

"Pity you can't eat them, which is even worse than paying so much of good money for a bunch of vegetables, Sade playfully nagged.

"Oh, you impossible witch," Frank contrived an agonized groan.

"Yes, I'm now going to cast a spell on you and make you take me to dinner," Sade purred.

"Yes, yes o wicked witch, I am under your evil spell. I will take you to dinner." Frank agreed with her.

•　　•　　•　　•　　•

A great film was showing that night at the Stratford cinema, and they decided to watch the film first, after which they went to Nando's; just a stone throw away. Sitting at a feast of flame-grilled chicken and baked potatoes, Frank had more than a bit of update for Sade.

"You mean you were arrested for a bank robbery?" Sade was incredulous.

"Yes, my dear," I knocked off a high street bank all by myself and the police let me off on good behavior," Frank told her.

"And before that, you lost your job; so how are you going to survive Frank? Not by weekend party gigs obviously."

"Not enough to sustain me honey; and I couldn't certainly afford you by doing weekend party gigs." he laughed

"So what are your plans, Frank?" Sade sounded genuinely worried for him.

"I was coming to that. Today I bought a detective course. I found that working as a detective isn't quite different from what I did as a journalist and it certainly looks like you could make a lot more in that business. Do you know that people actually fork out as much as a hundred and fifty pounds an hour to get a private detective?" Frank told her.

"Wow!" Sade sounded full of suspicion. "A hundred pounds an hour? I don't believe that."

"Better believe, because it's true. So I am going to start building myself a new and enduring profession honey."

"So what are you going to call yourself? What is your...erm...handle going to be like?"

"Handle? I am not a mug, sister."

"You are a really smart dummy you know; what are you going to call yourself? Under what handle will you be working...Sam Spade...Colin Fetchit? What is it going to be like? I personally am not going to employ Frank O'Dwyer to find even a lost cat.," Sade was sincere.

"Yeah, you've got a point there. I was thinking something like Frank Xero."

"Xero? That sounds awful."

"No it doesn't. Like a private investigator zeroes in on a crime and gets it solved real quick, gerrit?"

"Well, it's your business, not mine. It still sounds like a photocopy shop to me, like Xerox. Are you sure you aren't going to get sued by some of these business creeps in black suits?"

"Never worry Sade. On the positive side, it is going to make me easy to remember."

"No it's crappy, and I don't like it" Sade confessed "Try something more sensible like Frank Wire. It is also easy to remember I think. And it sounds rather cool. Like you are the new British werewolf – Frank Wire by day, MC Wire by night," she giggled.

"Hey what will I do without you, o witch" Frank nipped her ear with his teeth.

"Don't Snoop Dog me dude; not here" Sade pushed him away. "I think you are forgetting something though. Don't you need a license for this? "

"Not as far as I know," Frank told her. He had indeed checked earlier on his computer. Anyone with the wish could become a private detective.

Sade had updates of her own.

"I am happy for you then, and I hope you make a lot of money. I am participating in a fashion exhibition at the Barbican in a couple of weeks. It is an ethnic fashion show; I am so excited about the opportunity, Frank. It would be nice to have my designs break the ethnic barrier though. I am wishing for good contacts at the event," she told him.

"I love your designs SADE, especially the Dashiki tops. Trevor absolutely loves them too. I hope you are going to have a lot of them on display. Very nice to wear in summer." Frank encouraged.

"Yes, you both put a lot of business my way. I think it is time for me to break the ethnic barrier and something tells me the Barbican exhibition is going to be it, for me.," Sade was full of hopes.

"Go for it then, girl. You've got awesome talent in that lovely head of yours, and it is time for you to really make it big." Frank kissed her on the cheek. Sade put her arms around him.

"It's not only about the money though. I am proud of where I came from, and I would wish to change some unfortunate mindsets along the way. I aim to have elegant girls black and white, modelling exquisite Yoruba fashion like you've never seen before. For me, this will not be just another clothing exhibition; I want it to be a major cultural statement." Sade said.

"I believe you honey. I am sure one day; you will make a statement that will be heard and remembered all over the world." Frank said to her.

Together they went to the Sainsbury's supermarket for a couple of bottles of wine for the night.

CHAPTER 5

There had been more robberies than the bank job as Frank learned from the East End Mirror. A headline read: CAMCORDER ROBBERS STRIKE AGAIN.!

Pretty small time stuff all the robberies had been but done in the same insanely ridiculous way. A jewelry shop near Eastham got hit; they even did a pizza shop. The thought made Frank chuckle. A pizza shop getting knocked off; certainly looked very desperate to him. Somehow these stories could only be found in the East End Mirror, which Frank still dutifully read every day primarily in the hope that one day, the front page would contain a goodbye message announcing the demise of the newspaper, preferably due to the death of the proprietor, Spencer Cowley. Frank longed to be able to get rid of that dangling piece of his life – to see Spencer Cowley punished as the architect of his current unemployment situation.

But this never happened and the East End Mirror kept on. In any case, as Frank would wonder, East End Mirror was the only paper that reported these robberies, which gave the suspicion that something shady was afoot. Frank wondered whether Fernandez had at last strayed off the straight and narrow. But heck, the East End Mirror really wasn't his responsibility anymore. He didn't have a job with the East End Mirror anymore and therefore no business poking his nose into whatever went on there.

His payoff had dwindled very fast with bills knocking on his door daily. He had for a while swallowed his pride and tried a couple of those jobs he had previously rejected at the Jobcentre.

Frank tried the parking attendant job first, and it didn't last two weeks. He had quickly come in contact with some of the ugliest human beings in the world.

"I know where you live," a huge bricklayer had one afternoon told Frank as he snatched the ticket off his van, which had exceeded its time at a meter near Trinity Square Garden. The errant bricklayer's tree trunk size arms were covered with colorful serpent tattoos, and with a finger drawn menacingly across his throat, he emphasized his threat to Frank. The threat looked serious enough, but Frank wasn't going to make him believe that he was scared, so he flipped the man his middle finger, from twenty yards away, satisfied to see his jaw drop in both surprise and anger. Frank could feel the heat of the fellow's anger on him till he turned a corner into another street, and off to hand in his uniform and equipment. He certainly couldn't risk coming back here anymore.

Next, he took an easier job as a security guard at the local Tesco. It was a relatively easier beat, and Frank was stationed near the liquor shelves of the supermarket. It suggested that a lot of booze got stolen in these places, Frank would initially think. He also thought what a waste of time and money his mission was because any theft would occur between the innocent removal from the shelf and the dishonest non-payment at the check-out counter; the stolen item having disappeared in-between, into a large pocket or into an old lad lady's bag. It was a drudge job. He thought to give the Warden job at the underground a try next; at least he would get some fresh air all day. He now had a job again and could afford not to worry about many of his regular bills, but again he had this awful feeling that his life was again definitely going down the drain.

He got a call on his phone mid-day one extremely depressing Monday.

"Is this Frank Wire?" a husky voice came to him. Frank was initially confused. Then he remembered that he had paid for a classified advertisement to run in the Loot advertisement pages, and yes he was indeed the one advertised as Frank Wire, private detective.

"That's right sir, how may I be of help?" Frank replied with a show of importance.

My name is Harvey Simpson; I saw your advertisement for private investigation service."

"Yes that is what we do sir," Frank told him.

"Can you meet me in about one hour; I am at the Funky Munky. Do you know the place?

"The Funky Munky at Whitechapel I presume?"

"Yes, that is the one; you know it then?" Harvey Simpson seemed happy to learn this

Frank, of course, knew the Funky Munky; together with Trevor, he'd done a few gigs there, when it was still a dancing club and before it became a bar and restaurant.

"But I can't make it for the next two hours or so because I'm presently on a case," Frank told him.

"Never mind; I can still wait two hours "; Harvey Simpson said.

Frank felt a surge of excitement coming into his life again. He went to his supervisor and reported sick. She didn't look happy to hear that, but Frank wasn't interested in her happiness. Having thus relinquished his duty at Tesco for the day; he hopped on the bus for Whitechapel.

In the afternoon much of Whitechapel Road was a market, and you had to push and shove through a mass off bodies before you could get wherever you were going. Funky Munky was located in the block of houses which flanked the entire length of the market. It was a badly lit pub, and Frank found Harvey Simpson sitting at a table near the door, but not so near the glass front that the sun could reach him. Frank didn't know how he guessed that he would find him Harvey Simpson with a glass of Stout before him. Harvey didn't offer to buy him any. Frank nevertheless took a seat in front of Harvey and orders one too.

•　　•　　•　　•　　•

"Do you know my wife?" Harvey asked.

There was something Frank immediately found very disagreeable about this man. Not that he was a naturally evil person; far from it. Nevertheless, he had around him so miserable an aura which made him appear at least mildly schizophrenic. Indeed Harvey Simpson looked concurrently suicidal and homicidal. He certainly was not the kind of person Frank wanted to hang around having a drink with. In fact, he was not the kind of guy Frank wanted to work for. He was tempted to get up and walk away, but then remembered he'd worked for worse; he had worked for Spencer Cowley.

"Does this involve your wife them?" Frank asked needlessly.

"Yes it does, I think she's seeing another man," Harvey Simpson told him, his voice suddenly very weary.

"Another man such as her GP or maybe the mailman?" Frank tried to bring some laughter into his conversation, but Harvey Simpson merely scowled.

"Okay then, I think you want me to find out if he is seeing another man; like in having an affair, right?" Frank tried again.

"That's right, Harvey said. "Is that something you could do for me?"

"Of course yes, we do it every day. I've got four clients presently signed on," Frank told him.

"I want you to find out and bring me photographic evidence," Harvey said. Harvey wasn't interested in Frank's business.

"My rate is a hundred pounds an hour," Frank told him; "and this could take days you realize."

Harvey didn't look at him. He took out a roll of notes from his pocket, peeled off three fifties which he neatly folded and placed on the table.

"I will pay you three hundred for this job; and here is the deposit. I will pay you the balance when you deliver," he said to Frank. This was not even near what Mandy from Eagle Detective Agency had advised, but Frank guessed three hundred pounds was a good enough start.

"Okay, I will do this for you knowing how it feels like to have your partner cheat on you. I think we men should stick together," Frank said. Harvey didn't seem at all interested in Frank's fraternal opinion either. He nodded morosely and drank from his glass. Frank stood to leave but remembered that some question needed asking.

"How am I to know what your wife looks like when I find her?" he asked.

"I thought you'd never ask," Harvey replied with a malicious smile. He handed Frank an envelope. It contained a photograph and a slip of paper.

"That is a photograph of my wife, Ida. House address is on the paper; we live in Kentish Town."

Frank gave him a thumbs-up, disappeared the money into his coat pocket together with the envelope. He drank the rest of his beer, gave Harvey Simpson a thumbs-up, and left the Funky Munky.

CHAPTER 6

Ida Simpson wasn't anywhere near what anyone would call a beauty. In fact, she would just be so ordinary if not for those fantastic large eyes. About five-two, but she moved with unusual grace. She had been a clothes model, albeit a failed one, before she married Harvey Simpson, Frank would later learn.

Frank caught her leaving the house at Kentish Town the next morning about ten. She took the train to Tower station and then on to Dagenham, with Frank trailing along; safely out of her way and dressed up in workman's clothes. She was met at the station by a good looking young chap, who hugged her, and hand in hand they strolled away. Frank loitered for a long while around the shopping mall across the road while she and her friend had a lively chat and sandwiches in a coffee shop near the train station. Then they took a walk to a house, down a side lane off the main road. Frank presumed the house belonged to the dashing young bloke.

It wasn't a busy street and quite definitely, hanging around doing nothing would be quite suspicious. Someone could certainly get nervous enough to call the police. So Frank returned home, buying himself a cheap disposable camera and a pair of dark sunglasses at Dalston market. There he also found a tan fedora hat which looked great with the sunglasses. He initially thought against buying a raincoat to complete the outfit. He certainly didn't want to look like a detective from a fifties movie. But he eventually thought why not; seeing that he was going to be spending quite a bit of time outside and you never knew what the weather would be like in London. So he bought a dark raincoat also. The entire outfit looked glorious together.

Frank was better prepared for Ida Simpson next morning. He watched for her from a bus shelter where he sat, pretending to read a newspaper, and thanking his stars that he had bought the raincoat because it was indeed a very chilly morning.

Ida didn't come out of the house until well after twelve, and just as Frank was about to call it a day and return home. She was more reasonably dressed this day like she was going to the supermarket to get groceries. She spent much of the afternoon at a coffee shop in the mall having a chat with a party of old ladies. Frank was surprised that she indeed finally went to the supermarket to get groceries and go back home. There was nothing incriminating to report at all. Frank did a rethink of the ongoing situation. Maybe the bloke she met yesterday was just her brother. Maybe Harvey was a hallucinating case, which was not altogether impossible, on account of his drinking habit.

On the way home, Frank looked at himself in a shop window and thought he could do with a boost in self-confidence and self-esteem. So he went in and got his ears pierced and a couple of rings put in.

•　　•　　•　　•　　•

Frank understood he needed to work to his client's instructions which presently were to get proof for Harvey that his wife Ida was cheating on her. Nevertheless, what the heck did he know about human behavior? Nothing of which was ever like plain mathematics. People often did unbelievable things for even more unbelievable reasons, and when apprehended many even find it unbelievable that they did those things. So he went to have a discussion with Maureen at the Hard Luck Café.

"Maureen, how do you tell if a married person is having an affair?" He asked Maureen.

"How the heck am I supposed to know that? I have never been married. But I guess it would be fun though," Maureen replied.

"Fun to get married?" Frank asked. Maureen had never looked the marrying kind to him, he thought; but you never knew with women.

"No silly, fun to be having an affair while you are married," she laughed.

"That's nasty," Frank told her; truly disgusted.

"Oh you sensitive baby; sorry for hurting your feelings," she purred mischievously.

"That's alright, nothing personal," he told her; though he didn't think it was alright at all.

"So you've got someone having an affair? From what I learned when an affair begins, the mate that is cheating usually becomes more attentive to their spouse. Now that is not like I love you more thing, you understand; it is a guilt thing. Does that make sense?" Maureen told him.

"Yes, it does." Frank knew nothing about the relationship between Harvey and Ida Simpson, but he could visualize that pattern.

"Now after the affair is in full swing, the cheater begins to find constant fault with the spouse in an attempt to justify the affair in their mind. Again that is a guilt thing." he nodded; it made a lot of sense.

"Then the cheater begins to be a lot more attentive to the way they dress, bathes more frequent especially after returning home, pays more attention to physical fitness, and women especially tend to wear more perfume and a wider variety than usual. Does the person do any of these? "

"I wouldn't know, but I will check. That shouldn't be too difficult to find out."

"Sure," Maureen agreed. "Women additionally tend to have a "glow" about them when having an affair."

"Where did you get all these from Maureen?" Frank was as curious as he was impressed.

"Cosmopolitan magazine. A woman needs to be informed you know? You need to know what to watch out for in your husband to find out if the bastard is cheating out on you." She chuckled,

"And you need to know how to get your own back" she gleefully added:

•   •   •   •   •

Next day was luckier. Frank took pictures of the pair at the café; took pictures of them walking hand in hand and took pictures of them going into the house in Dagenham. This was a fantastic outing: for Frank. They were doing all the right things for him to report. Ida Simpson's goose was really cooked, he rejoiced. Next day, he would hand in the stuff and get the rest of his money from Harvey; case closed.

Frank was poised to take one showing the number on the door of the house when he heard steps behind him. There were four skinheads; all booted up.

"Oi, what you doing?" a tough kid with a rather deep voice grabbed him by the lapels. He looked like the leader of the pack

"Nothing," Frank shrugged.

"You wasn't doing nothing; you was taking pitchers," another from the pack said, his smile crooked, his eyes hostile and dangerous.

"Oh was I? Nasty habit isn't it?" Frank laughed nervously. They were not amused. The one who held his lapels went up to the door and hammered on it; while the other three fanned out behind as if determined to prevent Frank's escape. This wasn't going to be an easy escape he knew. They'd outrun him within thirty yards and probably beat him to a pulp.

Ida's friend popped his head out of the door, quite puzzled at the gathering.

"Hi Patchy, What's going on?" he addressed the leader.

"Bloke here was taking pitchers," the young hooligan, jerked his thumb in Frank's direction.

"Oh was he then; nice day for taking pictures, isn't it?" Asked Ida's friend, still very puzzled.

"Well, I was just generally admiring the neighborhood, and some butterflies and birds found around here; so yes I was taking some pictures. Nice day for taking pictures," Frank mustered up some courage.

"Liar, he was taking pitchers of you and your lady friend, he was," Patchy insisted. Ida's friend looked very nervous now. His discomfort increased when Ida came to the door herself, eyes quizzically looking at him.

"Would you like to come in for a moment?" Ida's friend asked Frank. He thought this a better option than being left to the mercy of the skinheads outside and quickly went inside.

"Okay Jimmy, we will stay outside for a bit in case you need us," Patchy assured.

• • • • •

The inside of Jimmy's house was sensibly furnished, and it looked nothing like a love nest. In the parlor the television was on and there on a table was a bottle of wine freshly cracked open, and which was all that suggested that anything that may be out of the ordinary was afoot. Jimmy went quickly over to the television and switched it off. Ida looked terribly worried.

"Why were you taking pictures of us?" Jimmy asked. He meant to sound menacing, but it didn't come out the way it ought to. He certainly was nowhere near a tough fellow. Handsome and fit, yes, but Frank felt sure he could drop this guy in fifteen seconds if they ever got in a fair fight. Nevertheless, this wasn't a fair fight situation. He had an unpredictable woman in front of him and four punks still hanging out by the door, waiting to tear me to pieces at her order

"He was? Jimmy, you said he was taking pictures of us?" "Ida uttered a distressed moan. "

"He certainly was. Patchy and the other chaps outside caught him doing it."

"Why were you talking our pictures?" Ida's voice was more unnerving. It sounded like the ascending growl of an angry wild cat.

"I was taking pictures of nature; landscape, butterflies, birds and all. I am a journalist. I don't know what those fools outside were on about." Frank tried to persuade her, but that only seemed to get her angrier.

Ida went to the ashtray on the table in which a smoldering cigarette laid unsmoked, the barrel half-burnt into a neat cylinder of grey ash. She picked up the cigarette, tapped off the ash with an angry finger and with such force that the cigarette snapped. Angrily she threw the rest in the ashtray, found a packet of Benson and Hedges and lit another one.

"Harvey sent you, didn't he?" It was more of an accusation than a question. Frank did the wise thing and remained silent. Jimmy snatched the camera from his hand dropped it on the floor and angrily stomped it to pieces, the effort driving a metal spring through the thin sole of his slippers into his foot. Jimmy yelled and hopped around a bit in pain. Frank suppressed his laughter.

"How much is he paying you?" Ida persisted.

"I told you I was taking pictures of butterflies. Who the heck is HARVEY for God's sake? Lady, I think you are mistaking me for someone else. I am a butterfly lover, not some pervert, going around peeking through keyholes."

. That came out alright until Jimmy, recovered from his foot injury yanked Frank's notebook from the pocket of his jacket.

"Give me that back," Frank protested, but Jimmy hopped a safe distance away, and from where he proceeded to flick through the notebook.

"Jesus, the bastard is a fucking spy, Ida. He's got your movement covered here for three days. He is even got me described. Looks like he works for fucking MI5!" Jimmy cried in alarm. "

"Let me see that," said Ida, snatching Frank's notebook from Jimmy. She flicked through the pages, humming "unh-unh," as each new page enlightened her about her life for the past three days. Her eyes were like fire when she was done. Frank fearfully backed away as she advanced. However, she suddenly stopped and quite nearly sagged.

"He plans to kill me. Did Harvey send you to kill me?" she sobbed. Frank emphatically shook his head.

"Listen, will you help me?" Ida said, looking quite beaten. "My life is in danger. Harvey is having an affair, with a woman he wants to marry after he has done me in. Will you help me? Please." Ida pleaded.

Frank was bewildered. Harvey too having his own little bit on the sly? Common sense told him however that this couldn't be true. The only affairs Harvey could manage would be with his beer: But then you never knew with married people.

"How much is he paying you to spy on me? How much? I will pay you more." Ida whined.

"He is paying me a thousand" Frank told her, now feeling more confident. Jimmy whistled in surprise.

"You are a fucking liar. You can't ever get a thousand quid out of Harvey, not for anything." Ida accused.

"Oh well, you can get any amount out of anybody if they are desperate enough to get anything," Frank tried to reason this out with her while congratulating her on how well she knew her husband. Ida seemed confused for a minute or two, angrily paced around the room, attacking her smoldering cigarette; and noisily exhaling the smoke like an angry drenched dragon.

"Alright, I will give you five hundred to follow Harvey and tell me where he goes every day," she said, snatching a roll of money from inside her bag and peeling off three hundred." I will give you the rest later when I get what you have."

"You said you will give me more. Harvey is giving me a thousand" Frank reminded her.

"I will give you five hundred," she said in a dangerous voice, her eyes angry and red hot. Frank pocketed the money.

"He broke my camera. How am I supposed to take photographs without my camera?"," Frank pointed at Jimmy who had been watching from afar, the entire situation having quite escaped him.

"It's a cheap shit anyway; costs three ninety-nine in the market," Jimmy laughed.

●　　　●　　　●　　　●　　　●

"Well, I didn't buy mine in the market. I bought it at Currys, and it cost me forty-nine ninety-five," Frank told Ida. She gave Frank ten pounds more. Frank tipped his hat to Ida, nodded to Jimmy, walked confidently out of the house and right through the four punks lolling outside. Having put a reasonable distance between himself and Jimmy's house, he turned into another street and fled for the train station. He had taken three hundred and ten quid from the suckers, and they hadn't even asked who he was and where he lived. He raced away, amused that the fools had no idea how and where to find him.

•   •   •   •   •

Frank arrived at the Hard Luck Café about an hour later and ordered sausages, mashed potatoes and a glass of orange juice. While he ate, he also read the day's edition of the East End Mirror. The paper was to his annoyance actually perking up. He couldn't recognize most of the by-lines anymore, but this was perfectly understandable because they were fake names anyway. When he still worked with the newspaper, it was usual to have at least a dozen of those names at hand, to give the impression of a huge staff. Today the paper had no news that mattered.

Frank got the call from Raj Desai after finishing his lunch. Raj Desai was Indian, as the name and voice suggested.

"This is the detective?" the caller seemed to accuse.

"Yes, my name is Frank Wire, private detective," Frank agreed.

"Good, good. You will meet me this afternoon, no? I have important discussion with you."

"I am quite busy, but I will squeeze you into my schedule. Hang on a minute while I look at my diary," Frank told him. He quietly hummed for half a minute to give an impression

"Okay, how does three o clock sound?" Frank finally asked. Raj Desai agreed to see him at three o clock.

"You will meet me at my shop Bhatti's at Upton Park, no?" Raj suggested.

CHAPTER 7

Frank found Bhatti's exactly where Raj had said it would be, located about a hundred yards away from the tube station. It was a large and busy shop filled with mostly African and Asian customers. A million miles of gold and silver chains were displayed on mounted reels around the shop; so did stones of every description twinkle merrily, gaudily from dozens of racks scattered around the shop. Raj met Frank at the door and led him to an office located at the back. It was just a cubicle about four feet by six deep and much of the space occupied by a table.

"Come, come in and take a seat" Raj suggested.

"Take a seat? This place is hardly large enough to swing a cat" Frank joked. Raj did not look amused.

"Why do you want to swing a cat?" he humorlessly inquired.

"Just my little joke; it's a figure of speech"; Frank waved it off. Raj still didn't appear to get it.

"My shop was burgled last week. Do you know anything about it?" Raj asked. Frank was genuinely surprised.

"Why should I know anything about it?"

"You are a detective, no?"

"Of course, I am a detective, not the god Buddha."

"Very funny, very funny indeed," Raj said; not laughing at all.

"Anything of value missing then? I am sure you called me here for a purpose," Frank asked.

"Yes, yes I was coming to that. Some men came into my shop carrying a television camera. They told me they were from BBC and making a program of my shop. Only they did not make a program. They went away with a lot of my money and jewelry."

"I have seen this before"; Frank laughed. Raj looked bewildered.

"You have seen it before? I ask if you if you know about the burglary and you say no. Now you have seen it before."

"What I mean is that I have seen this sort of trick done before. A bank was robbed in the same way, and I was there in the bank."

"You robbed a bank with a camera. How is that possible?"

"I did not rob a bank with a camera; I saw some people rob the bank with a camera, in the same way, that your shop was robbed." Raj Desai now looked very much unimpressed with Frank; the ear-rings which Frank wore lending more distrust.

"I don't understand you at all; are you sure you are a detective?"

"So you want me to recover your lost money and jewelry then. How much money was stolen?"

"Never mind the money; after they went away, I looked for an important item, and it was also missing. It is a lucky charm. They must have taken it away."

"So you want me to recover the lucky charm. What does it look like?"

Raj took out the empty velvet case. It now only contained an image which was printed on a small piece of parchment paper.

"It is called The Crooked Bullet," Raj said. The image did look like a curved bullet or a banana. Heck, to Frank it looked like a bent dick.

"It looks like a bent dick," he said.

"Bent dick, bent bullet; it does not matter. What it matters is that my life will suffer if I don't find that lucky charm again. My business is suffering already because of this. Yesterday I did not make many sales. I want you to find the lucky charm for me as soon as possible."

Frank was not a great believer in superstition, but the money which this promised to bring his way, he quite loved.

"I charge a hundred pounds an hour," Frank told Raj.

Raj looked at him for a long minute as if trying to read his mind and not succeeding. He took out a wooden case, opened it and brought out a medallion which dangled from a long chain.

"Look at this one. The stolen charm also hangs from a chain such as this" Raj said, as he swung the medallion like a pendulum in front of Frank's face. Frank was initially puzzled but in a moment found himself becoming hypnotized by the swinging medallion. Shaking his head to recover control, he stood and pushed. Raj fell against the wall, bounced off and fell upon the table.

"What the heck are you trying to do, you idiot?" Frank asked.

"Very sorry, I was trying to find out if you are really a detective. I don't want to give money away to a fake detective," Raj uneasily tried to explain.

"Do I look anything like a fake detective to you?" Frank growled. Raj nodded, silently.

"Think whatever you like, but this will cost you ten thousand pounds," Frank said. "To find your lost lucky charm will cost you ten thousand pounds."

"You guarantee to find it for me?"

"It might take a bit of time, perhaps a couple of weeks; but I am able to find it."

"How will you find it then?" still very suspiciously.

"I am a detective. There are several ways to skin a cat."

"You do not like cats?" Raj asked after a long minute.

"Never mind; it is just a figure of speech. I mean there are several ways to arrive at the same result."

"Ten thousand is a lot of money, no?"

"It's a lot of work," Frank told him.

The door opened and in stepped a young lady whom Frank thought had hostile thoughts for him immediately and for absolutely no reason.

"Ah Rupinder, come meet Mister Frank Wire; he is a private detective," Raj said to the lady. She nodded without a word. Frank offered his hand. Rupinder declined to shake.

"Private detective is going to help me find the missing charm," Raj explained. Rupinder remained silent; merely stared at Frank for a long while as if trying to memorize his face.

"Okay daddy, just dropped in to say hello. See you later"; she finally said before leaving. Raj sat again; he took out a checkbook, wrote on it; tore out a check for Frank. It was for two thousand pounds. Frank found himself fighting like crazy to contain his excitement.

"You get the rest when you find my lucky charm," Raj said.

Frank left Raj's office whistling, with the check in his hand and also with a photocopied image of the lost pendant. He thought he had much to whistle about; twenty-five hundred pounds earned in a week wasn't beans.

•　　•　　•　　•　　•

Alone again in the office, Raj sadly and quietly bore the brunt of his deceased wife's scowl from the portrait on the wall. It was a scowl which at this time told him: See what you have done now Raj, I always said you were no good, didn't I? Now you have gone and lost the shop's money and also got your lucky thing pinched. Shame on you, Raj.

On the way back home, Frank stopped at a Sainsbury's and bought himself two bottles of wine, a six pack of Guinness and half a dozen frozen Chinese dinners. He popped one of the frozen dinners in the microwave, cracked open a can of Guinness, and as he ate his chow mien, he wondered how he would find Raj Desai's damned lucky charm.

•   •   •   •   •

Trevor came to pick him up around ten at night. He had dozed off but was soon ready to go. He donned his favorite black bowler hat, a plain black t-shirt, the heavy neck chain, and rings. And MC-Wire was ready to go. The gig that night was their regular Friday night engagement at Skeleton Screw Club on Old Street. As usual, the equipment had been moved in by a guy named Heavy Dee; a surly Jamaican friend of Trevor's and whom Frank didn't particularly like. Frank had to be nice to Heavy Dee nevertheless because Heavy Dee owned the equipment. Heavy Dee also desperately wanted to join up with them, and Trevor had been sort of playing him along. Heavy Dee didn't know rhythm from risotto, but he tried desperately to learn nevertheless.

Trevor had come in a new black BMW which looked out of this world.

"Nice ride you nick it?" Frank had joked. He had been quite thrown when Trevor told him that he, in fact, bought it. It really looked an expensive car, and Frank would later check the going cost on the Internet, and find that it did cost a fortune. Trevor indeed had a job at Newham Council offices, plus he had a little event promotion business on the side so he could afford to make payments on a car, but a thirty thousand quid ride did seem a bit out of a reasonable income bracket. Frank had for a minute wondered if Trevor was dealing on the side, but dismissed the idea. Trevor was a clean cookie didn't smoke, didn't drink and was vegetarian.

A smooth and moving piece was playing on the car stereo. It sounded like Herbie Hancock doing Barry White with a synthesized voice. He recognized the track from Ex-Man's new record. He would think again that despite the heavily electronic vocal, there persisted the feeling that the voice sounded familiar. But then why shouldn't it? Even Trevor was doing imitation at their gigs; so were a dozen other deejays around London and perhaps several hundred around the world.

"Hey, that shit is from the Ex-Man's new record. Great stuff. As usual it's got lots of heavily synthesized vocals, but believe me, despite that, I keep getting the feeling the voice behind it all sounds familiar.," Frank said.

"Why shouldn't it sound familiar? I have been playing Ex-Man stuff at our gigs for some months now. So have several hundred other deejays around the world." Trevor laughed.

"You're right. Almost everyone in England is hooked on Ex-Man. Terribly unique style. It is mostly about the mystery appeal though. Faceless musician doing contemporary remixes of seventies hits. Genius!" Frank agreed,

It was true: almost everyone in England now raved-up on Ex-Man these days. Not that he had a style that was terribly unique. Only that the faceless musician had this knack of remixing seventies songs and adding a contemporary translation to them, to make them feel, so fresh. It wasn't only that, there was this x-ingredient that he did always infuse into the entire arrangement - like the secret ingredient in the druid's soup which made stars explode from inside the soup. Yes, Ex-Man did have the X-factor in his funky bag. The piece playing was, in fact, a re-do of Barry White's "Let The Music Play," with the thudding bass racing alongside a snare drum; above the entire arrangement, a smooth rap took firm control, while a rolling baritone voice urged from the background:

"Right on—Right on—Right on,"

"Right on—right on—right on" Trevor sang as he fingers tapped on the car steering.

"Right on—right on—right on. Frank sang along.

CHAPTER 8

Spencer Cowley sat in the conservatory of his home, staring at the empty bird cage, hanging from a hook near the garden exit. His mind went back five years when he had a bird in that cage. It was a beautiful creature with shiny yellow and rust feathers. He would every day bring to that bird, seeds, nuts, worms, bugs and all the good things he felt a bird could ever desire. And for him, this bird would sing and twitter beautifully; gratefully.

One day, Spencer thought to give the happy bird a little bit more roaming space, and so he took the cage outside and flung open its gate. The little bird first appeared at a loss, like he didn't trust Spencer's motive. It hopped toward the open gate, and there it stood for a long while contemplating the wide expanse of freedom that had suddenly become obtainable. It hopped a little distance away from its dungeon and again paused as if not believing its great fortune. Then with a leap and a powerful burst of flapping wings, it fled into the sky with all its might never again to return. Spencer remembered being sad for days. He'd actually believed that the bird genuinely loved him; he'd actually believed that the bird's songs were of love.

• • • • •

Spencer's thoughts switched back to the problem he presently had in hand, and it concerned a fellow called Fred Duffy. He'd met Fred three months back. Spencer remembered the first time Fred came visiting. He had also been sitting in the conservatory when the front doorbell rang. He knew who it was, but his wife Susan had gone to open the door before he could get up. It was Frank Duffy, the man he had been expecting.

"Good evening, I am here to see Mr. Spencer Cowley," he heard Fred Duffy tell Susan. His wife's response was pleasant but suspicious. Susan knew it wasn't usual for her husband to bring friends or business home.

"What is this about? Who are you?" Susan asked.

"My name is Frederick Duffy. I spoke to him on the phone earlier." Fred explained himself.

Susan called Spencer to announce the visitor; Spencer came to the front door to lead Fred Duffy to the conservatory.

"How are you Fred? At last, we meet. Do sit down. Would you like a beer Fred? Of course, you must; every man must like a beer at least once a while." He brought Fred a can of beer from the fridge and one for himself, disregarding Susan's disapprovingly. Look in his direction.

"You live here in Barking, isn't that right Fred?" Spencer asked

"That is quite right. I live a quarter of a mile away from you. I only came here about six months ago though, from Southampton. I am a sociology lecturer at the University of East London as I previously told you. "Fred enthusiastically told him.

"Interesting. What took you then to the Yahoo Murder and Mystery Internet Group? Was the interest related to your work?" Spencer asked. Fred Duffy nodded.

"I run a very interesting course called Criminal Psychology. It is very popular with the students. I try to spice the lectures up with an interesting crime anecdote now and then. The students love it.," Fred said

"Yes I can quite understand why they do; we live in a very criminal world don't we? Politicians, police, business organizations, robbers; you never really can tell the difference anymore, can you? I mean they all look the same these days." Spencer laughed.

.Yes, a very criminal world; a very mad world too." Fred nodded.

"Fred, I own a newspaper as you already know. Plus I do a bit of freelance scriptwriting for a television crime and mystery series. You know Murder Zone?" Spencer asked.

"Yes, I do know that program. I also watch it all the time. I think the plots are great; I didn't know you were part of the team" Fred Duffy was truly awed

"That is quite flattering Fred, thank you. I do like my plots to come out of real life; I try to make them as believable as possible. I have reporters on the roll of my newspaper who give me enough incidents and scenarios every week to keep me busy, and that is why the producer loves my work. But it seems like the world has become used to gruesome murders as a way of life and television movies may soon lose appeal. I have this project that I am working on nevertheless. It is my own television reality show. It is going to give the audience the opportunity to plot and execute a murder by themselves. I think it will be a huge hit," Spencer proudly announced.

"Hmmn...that sounds interesting. Tell me more?" Fred encouraged.

"It is a game really and like I said I think it could make a great serial. But beyond all these, it would also generate some exciting plots for my work with Murder Zone. "

"That makes economic sense. Killing two birds with one stone is never a bad idea" Fred agreed.

"I was looking for someone to test the game out with, and that was how I found you. It is always a bad to take a half-baked television proposal to the market, as you probably don't know. .I have temporarily called my television game Just Dessert, and this is how it is played. : For a million pounds or so, the contestants look at the best means of killing a fictitious person without the crime being discovered. Like Who Wants To Be A Millionaire for a world full of sociopaths. He may even call a friend if he gets stuck" Spencer explained.

"Doesn't look too difficult, does it? Newspapers all over the world are full of unsolved murders." Fred laughed

"That is what you think. But try polishing the person up. For example, give the man a great family and a playful dog, and it gets more difficult as you go along" Spencer told Fred.

"Not for a lunatic" Fred honestly replied.

"Well we wouldn't want to have lunatics participating in this show, would we? This game will be played by ordinary people like you and I. The objective is to be able to get an insight into the mind of the ideal murderer – the one who kills without compassion." Spencer explained.

"Yes, I can understand that. Those are certainly creatures that the world needs to understand. Why do they do it? Nobody apparently knows for sure" Fred nodded.

"So what do you say we meet once every other week and create some scenarios together? I am sure this will also enrich your lectures." Spencer suggested as Fred drank the rest of his beer.

"There exists such a possibility; it looks like a nice idea. Look, Spencer, I just thought to drop in for a few minutes, and I need to go right now. There is a football match this afternoon at Upton Park. Are you a football person?" Fred asked him, getting to his feet.

"No, I am quite the agoraphobic type. That is what my kind of work turns you into, isn't it? How does next Sunday at five sounds to you then?" "Spencer grinned.

"Lovely, I'll see you then Spencer. Bye." Fred said as Spencer let him out at the front door.

•   •   •   •   •

Fred was back next Sunday as agreed, and this time Spencer opened the front door to let him in.

" Ah! There you are Fred; quite a punctual fellow you are then. Come right in. Let me introduce you to my wife. Susan, meet Fred, he teaches at the university," Susan said a stiff hello.

"How are you today, Susan?" Fred heartily asked

"Quite well I think. I have to run along now. Spencer, I will be upstairs if you need me" Susan said before leaving them. Frank led Fred to the conservatory.

"So where do we begin Spencer? Who do we kill first?" Fred chuckled.

"You are really a proper bloodthirsty monster aren't you? Yes, I like that approach Fred - get into the mind of the murderer. Who do I kill next? I've got a man in mind. He is eighty-five years old; living together with his wife, seventy-nine. They are really two adorable dinosaurs. His name is Dennis Snow, and his wife is Maria." Spencer said as he returned from the fridge with two cans of beer and glasses."

"She's Italian?" Fred asked.

"Maybe she is; does it matter?" Spencer shrugged

"If her brother is a Mafia guy, it of course matters." Fred laughed

"No, she's actually a proper English wife; she does some senseless knitting all day too." Spencer shook his head,

"Geriatricide shouldn't be considered much of a crime though. To me, it should be like euthanasia -, a mercy service to the poor souls." Fred said. Again Spencer shook his head.

"But that is not how it is in this case. Dennis Snow is a WWII Nazi concentration camp survivor. He's got a bit too much of military information in his noggins, and the information is so hot that it's making some people uneasy. And they figure the earlier Dennis the Menace goes to sleep the better for them. So how do we get this one done then?" Frank said

"Well, first of all, where does he usually go and what does he go to do there? What are his usual schedules if he has any?" Fred asked

"That will be the frustrating part. Here is the background. Dennis Snow goes nowhere. His schedule is to sit in a chair all day and stare like a gecko. God, I am going to hate old age Fred. What about you?" Spencer grimaced.

"Very true; who the heck wants to get old and end their life in a home. About Dennis Snow though, let me think."

"Go ahead we have all evening. I will get you another beer," Spencer encouraged. And so had the discussion gone late into the night.

•　　•　　•　　•　　•

Spencer had been very surprised at how easily Fred caught on with the game. He thought this was a good sign that the game should not be too difficult for both participants and audience to understand. He also decided y there was nothing much to understand. The game had three participants: the client, the contractor and the investigator. The client, who would be the presenter, brought in a job; might be a robbery, fraud, murder, a job with a moral motive. He gave it to the contractor, and there may be a group of them if you like. The contractor would now look for the best means to carry out the crime, the objective being that it must be unsolvable. It would now be left to the investigator, who might either be another participant or the audience, to unravel the crime. Discussing with Fred Duffy revealed to him nevertheless how tough it was to kill a good person and also avoid discovery.

•　　•　　•　　•　　•

"I don't like strange people coming into the house Spencer. If he wants beer, let him go get it at a pub. Please don't start bringing stray dogs into my house," Susan had told Spencer later the next week, after Fred had left. She did look angry as she said that.

"He's assisting me to work on my project, Susan. Come on give me a break," Spencer was also in no mood to agree with her, even though he understood the futility of arguing with his Susan

"I don't want an argument with you Spencer. I just don't like that man. He drinks too much for one thing." Susan persisted.

"No problem Susan; I'm buying the beer and not you, so why get yourself upset over nothing. "Spencer took a bold stand.

"That's another problem Spencer. You're not supposed to be drinking, and you are not supposed to smoke anymore. Dr. Maxwell warned you about that you know" Susan sighed. Spencer found himself fighting desperately to put his rising temper under control.

He'd become depressed two years back. The whole weight of the many challenges and disappointments he faced at work had sent him into a drinking binge and finally into psychiatric care for a couple of months.

"That was a long time Susan. I'm okay now. All I had was a bit of a stress situation. The thing about doctors is that they always exaggerate your situation just to make themselves feel so important. I mean do I look like I'm a nut?" he said

"You are not a nut Spencer. I am just concerned. My intuition tells me that this man is likely to get us into trouble, and I think you should get rid of him." Susan told him.

But Spencer had no intention of agreeing with Susan on this and was quite glad that Susan eventually let go of that particular battle.

•   •   •   •   •

Two weeks later, Spencer was again having the usual Sunday evening conversation with Fred in the conservatory, and the topic still remained about the old man, Dennis Snow and his wife.

"I still don't believe we have not been able to nail Dennis Snow for weeks" Spencer wondered

"It really beats me too Spencer. Eighty-five year old guy; lame and never gets out of his wheelchair.One would have thought this is a job for a one-armed monkey." Fred chuckled.

"Well, we do have an unusual situation, don't we? This old guy has a wife who hangs around him all day long like his bad breath." Spencer sighed...

"This nutty woman is putting us in a fix Spencer. I mean she just hangs around the guy, doing her senseless knitting. She is a big problem Spencer. I think we should do her too." Fred laughed

"No, the client wouldn't have that." Spencer disagreed.

"In that case, why don't we just get the old lady to do the dirty job? She could slip some poison into his tea or something."

"No. Maria loves her husband. Apart from that, she's an amateur with poisons. We need a clean job."

"Send in a psycho to ransack the house, beat the old girl up a little bit and then do the guy."

"She's likely to scream and bring the neighbours running."

"Well, I give up. Why don't we just wait for the guy to drop dead? Hasn't got very long to go anymore is the way I see it" Fred finally submitted.

"The client cannot wait. The situation is that there is a secret to protect, and if it ever gets out it's going to cost the client a lot." Spencer persisted.

"How about a good clean headshot with a long-range rifle" Fred tried again.

"No chance. Remember Dennis Snow never goes outside. Never comes near the windows. He's probably got mildew growing on his butt already. It will make more sense to have the killer climb through the window and fix him with a silenced handgun."

"Hire a retired SAS then." Fred again desperately tried.

"Are you out of your nut? How the hell does one hire SAS to do a murder? And remember anyway that Maria is always with him. The wife must not be killed or hurt." Spencer reminded him.

"Well, she certainly must have to leave him by himself for some minutes. At least she would need to make his tea. That is a perfect opportunity to nail him, in and out in a minute or two." Fred triumphantly declared.

And that was how they had left it. But Spencer had made up my mind what to do with Dennis Snow; only he hadn't told Fred. And he thought that was what made Just Desserts an interesting game.

●　　●　　●　　●　　●

Their exciting discussion was this night cheerfully interrupted by Susan

"Dinner is ready Spencer. Would you fancy a bite too, Mr. Duffy?" She asked.

Your dinner certainly smells better to me." Fred Duffy thanked her

"Let's close this case Fred. It is an impossible job." Spencer decided

"Terrific meal, Mrs. Cowley. I haven't had anything like this since my wife passed on five years ago." Fred Duffy said after dinner.

"I am sorry to hear that. What was the matter with her?" Susan was certainly concerned,

"She'd been unwell for several years; something about her pancreas. It was a very bad time for her, and I really do feel thankful that she went even though I'd rather still have her with me. She was in great pain." Fred sadly told her.

"Oh, you poor man. You live alone then?" Susan felt so sorry. Fred nodded.

"I never could really think there is anyone able to replace her. She was to me a mother, wife, friend and the most marvellous cook in the world. Since she left, I now just drink my dinner from a bottle most nights. Your cooking is quite wonderful too Mrs. Cowley. I especially like this dessert. What is it called?"

"You nice man; it is peach cobbler. Spencer loves cobblers; don't you Spencer?" Susan laughed, enjoying the compliment.

"Oh yes, cobblers are nice," Spencer replied without emotion.

"This peach cobbler was certainly lovely." Fred truthfully said as he got up. "Well, I do have to go now. Thank you again for the meal, Mrs. Cowley. Hope I get invited again next time.

"You are certainly welcome Fred. Goodnight." Susan gushed.

•   •   •   •   •

Spencer saw Fred to the door and thereafter returned to sit in the parlour with Susan. He pretended to watch television with Susan.

"He was very smooth, wasn't he?" Spencer hesitantly said.

"I beg your pardon" Susan replied, genuinely nonplussed

"I mean Fred. All that story about his dead wife. Like he was really trying to worm his way into your heart, and I guess he succeeded. Really smooth of him." Spencer repeated.

"Don't tell me you are getting jealous Spencer. He's your friend, isn't he? He just looks so lonely is all I see. Obviously misses his wife very much. Obviously still loves her so much too." Susan laughed.

"Jealous? Don't be ridiculous. Why should I be jealous?" Spencer sulked.

•   •   •   •   •

Somehow however things changed quite distastefully since that night. Susan had greeted Fred with a warm hug next time he came visiting. And from then on. Spencer could see that an irritating sort of interaction began to develop between Fred and Susan. Spencer also noticed that Fred became more careful with his dressing. The usual sweatshirt was replaced by a nice dinner jacket and a neck scarf. And oh, how he stank of Brut. Susan also generally became sunnier whenever Fred visited. Gone was the characteristic coldness by which Spencer sometimes sensed her presence about the house during Fred's earlier visits. And oh, she also dressed especially for those evenings with Fred. And as far as Spencer believed, when a woman wore high heels around the house, you get the impression that she's partying, And Spencer wondered why women did such crazy things such as this."

•   •   •   •   •

Dinner with Fred Duffy and Susan had been quite an infuriating event, the Sunday after.

"Exquisite dinner as usual Susan; and also a wonderful dessert." Fred, as usual, congratulated Susan.

; It was trifle this time just in case you didn't notice. Spencer doesn't really care about food most days; isn't that true Spencer? I remembered you mentioned that you loved trifle, Fred." Susan purred.

"Yes, I certainly love trifle. I wouldn't trifle with trifle. It always hits my weak spot. Ever since I was a kid you could kill me with trifle," Fred chuckled.

"I did try to liven it up with a splash of rum. But I guess with what you boys have put away in the last couple of hours of trying to kill people that don't exist; you probably wouldn't feel any of that rum." Susan laughed

"Yes, I did notice. I thought it was just rum flavour though." Fred affirmed

As was beginning to become the routine, Spencer felt to his unspoken fury completely removed from these conversations. One thing that he enjoyed though about these bizarre dinner events was that, whenever Fred came visiting dinner was good. The dessert was always very good. Oh, he'd never seen Susan put so much care and love into preparing dessert. And Spencer was sure Fred had never had good meals like he did on Sunday nights at his house. To his horror he had even a few times noticed Fred's eyes following Susan all about the house like a very hungry dog at a sausage parade. And Spencer could imagine the intention behind those looks. They were the sort of look which told him it may be just a matter of time for that lady to become the dessert - like as soon as his back was turned and the realization made him very angry.

●   ●   ●   ●   ●

"I have finally concluded Snow, Fred. The problem is solved. It so happened that Snow killed his wife Maria first, just before the assassin struck." Spencer told Fred Duffy, while they had coffee in the conservatory, after dinner.

"Dennis Snow is eighty-five for Christ sake. How would he do a hell of a thing like that?" Fred was astonished.

"Oh, she brought him weak tea; and while she's turning away, he bludgeoned her to death with the tea kettle," Spencer said.

"You are out of your mind."

"Hey, you never know with men. He's been married for over sixty years, and this wife has been hanging around him and nagging his ass off for sixty years Fred. Perfect reason, isn't it? Snow contemplated spending his last few years alone and in bliss. "Spencer shrugged.

"You seem quite pleased to have that old lady dead, aren't you? I thought she wasn't to be hurt." Fred Duffy was genuinely sorry to learn

"Well, death happens. She unfortunately died. The assassin had nothing to do with this one." Spencer contrived his sadness.

●   ●   ●   ●   ●

Susan's accident had happened the next Sunday. She'd been dressing up when the doorbell rang; definitely Fred. She hurriedly started to descend the stairs and came tumbling down. She was not moving when Spencer got to where she was lying at the foot of the stairs. Spencer took off her shoes, looked mischievously at the broken high heels before going away to chuck them in the bin. After letting Fred in, he called for an ambulance, which came to take Susan away to the hospital.

Contemplating the extent of the danger he could have also put himself in, gave Spencer cold sweat. He had only hoped that she would sprain her ankle or something like that, but it was a really nasty fall Susan had taken. She got herself concussion, and fractured arm and leg. Only if she had been more careful when descending stairs; only if she had known that she was wearing high-heeled shoes, which someone had tampered with the high heels.

"I am hurting. Spencer; I am hurting all over. I wish I was dead." Susan moaned in her hospital bed. She did look an awful sight with legs and arms in plaster, and one of her legs strung up.

"Hush. I wish you would stop saying that Susan; you don't look that bad yet. Never mind, you will be out of here in no time." Spencer encouraged.

"Have you been taking your medicine Spencer? Dr. Maxwell says it is very important that you take them," Susan asked from deep within her haze of pain.

"Those pills only make me groggy and disjointed Susan, but sure I've been taking them." Spencer lied.

"Dr. Maxwell also said that it is important for you to stay away from alcohol and smoking. Please do that for me Spencer," she pleaded.

"Stop talking this way Sue. Anyone would think you were at death's door already. Believe me, I'm okay now. What I had was a bit of stress situation I keep telling you. Doctors tend to exaggerate things." Spencer's anger threatened again to get out of control.

"Just be careful," Susan whispered, finally falling asleep.

●　　　●　　　●　　　●　　　●

Spencer found Fred Duffy waiting in the hospital lobby, sitting in a chair. Fred got up and approached him. He looked so distraught.

"Poor Susan. On the brighter side though, it is lucky she didn't break her neck when she fell down those stairs." Fred said.

"Yes very lucky for me," Spencer agreed, a chilling wave coursing through his entire body.

"I mean worse could have happened. Poor girl could have died," Fred persisted.

"Yes, very lucky for her." Spencer agreed

●　　　●　　　●　　　●　　　●

It is lucky she didn't break her neck when she fell down those stairs

Again, that thought made Spencer feel very uncomfortable. He had nearly killed Susan, and that would have been a pretty big mess, wouldn't it? It wouldn't be hard to imagine the police machinery getting hold of the offending shoe. It wouldn't be hard at all to imagine the police machinery sniffing around in the neighbourhood. And, it wouldn't be hard at all for them to soon learn that Susan and husband were sometimes not such great friends. Not very hard at all, to see what their conclusion would have been. He had just barely escaped spending the rest of his life in prison.

CHAPTER 9

When he inherited money from a person he had never met, the man known as Moses Samuel had his entire life turned upside down. Two hundred and fifty million pounds would do worse to a lot of people. Suddenly he found that he did not have to work again for the rest of his life, which was a drag for an able-bodied and very active forty-two year old. Twenty years back or forth, he could have been able to embark on a crash and burn life mission – like investing a substantial part of his money on a drugs and booze binge, or catching himself a twenty-year-old sexpot. But the forties were a time of life in which you begin to be seriously aware of and oddly very fearful of your mortality.

The farm which he renamed Woodstock was part of the inheritance. On the wings of a long-time fantasy, he had turned the farm into a health spa with quite eccentric rules even by health spa standards. He had known Sasha Cohen a couple of decades from a regular writers" group meet-up in a Bond Street pub. They had become very close, but were not lovers, since Sasha was not into men. And so when Moses Samuel needed someone with enough imagination to match his own, he had reunited with Sasha and had never regretted this.

Not forgetting his rough upbringing in the jungle of Peckham and the extremely demanding job he had before this windfall happened to him, Moses Samuel had decided to put some of the money into a fund to help people of talent.

How had he located Ex-Man's hidden transmitter and consequently Ex-Man? For a man of sufficient means, locating amateur broadcasting equipment wasn't so great an achievement. Having done this, and having found who the Ex- Man was, he finally decided to invite him for a little chat. This afternoon, sitting alone in his office; admiring his collection of African artifacts and portraits, he smiled mischievously, picked up his phone and dialed a number.

"Is this the Ex-Man?" Moses Samuel confidently asked when the phone answered

"Sorry you've got the wrong number." the person on the other end replied after a long pause and then hanged up. Smiling, Moses Samuel redialed the number.

"What is your problem? Don't you understand English? I just told you it's a wrong number," the receiver angrily scolded.

"Hold on a minute and listen to me. I know who you are; I know where you live. I am prepared to let these remain your secret, even though a million of your fans all over the world would die for that information.," Moses Samuel calmly replied.

"What do you want?" the receiver replied with a deep sigh. The game was up, he admitted; his greatest hope being this call was not from the police.

"Nothing that you can't give. Actually, you have so much to gain by listening to what I have to say to you. I am not law enforcement by the way," Moses Samuel said.

"Screw the bullshit. What do you want?" the fellow seemed again to regain some more confidence.

"I have a proposition for you. I will be at Trinity Square Garden at six this evening; only me. I will be wearing a black coat, no hat; no hair."

"And why do you think, I will be there? I don't need whatever you may be offering. Go screw yourself," the man sneered. But Moses Samuel remained calm.

"See you at six. I will be standing by the memorial at Trinity Square Garden.," he said and thereafter cut the phone.

●   ●   ●   ●   ●

Later in the evening, Moses Samuel emerged from the Tower Hill tube station, walked into the garden; and standing by the war memorial, made a show of studying the inscribed names. He was soon joined by a black male, wearing dark glasses and his coat lapel turned up to obscure most of his face and head.

"Continue with what you're doing. Don't turn to look at me or I am out of here in two seconds. Now, what do you want from me?" the black guy said to him in a low voice.

"Don't get so difficult. I am sure after I've said my piece, you'll love me more." Moses Samuel obeyed

"Go ahead; I am listening. And you'd better not be wasting my time here." Ex-Man told him. Moses Samuel sighed deeply and introduced himself.

"My name is Moses Samuel. I have not always been known by that name though. I used to be a journalist who stepped on a lot of toes, I also in the course of my career made some people proud to be human beings. I loved my job. One day I learnt that a very wealthy man had left me a lot of money in his will; two hundred and fifty million pounds to be exact. I suddenly found that I did not have to work again for the rest of my life. I was still a very active thirty-eight-year-old man. Twenty years back or forth, I could have become a very confused person, but you know what I did? I bought myself a farm in Chigwell which I converted into a health spa for the rich. My place is called Woodstock."

"I know the place; I've been there a couple of times with a friend. It's a good place." Ex-Man said.

"Good. I hope the story gets better from this point. I grew up rough in Peckham, and I am really unable to forget the extremely demanding job I had before my windfall; so I also decided to put some of the money into a fund to promote people and causes that could improve humanity.," Moses Samuel said. Ex-Man impatiently flicked his hand, urging Moses Samuel to get on with the story.

"That's cool. I will make it brief too. I have a music concert coming up soon, and I am looking for a star musician." Moses Samuel continued.

"Wait a minute should it not be the other way round? I mean doesn't it make more sense to find your so-called star musician and then you have a concert? I am sure. That's the way it is done." Ex-Man chuckled

"Quite correct. In this case however, it can't be done any other way. I like you and want you to star in my concert. Indeed it will be your concert - about you. I am afraid it may also be the end of anonymity for you, but for that, I am able to pay handsomely," Moses Samuel offered.

"And what if I tell you to go fuck yourself?" Ex-Man wasn't about to be so easy.

"You will be perfectly within your rights to say that, but I am hoping you wouldn't.," Moses Samuel nodded. Ex-Man seemed lost in thought for several minutes.

"What's the catch? I mean you are no promoter as far as I know and apparently the money from this doesn't mean anything to you. And as far as this looks, I am the only person who stands to profit. So, what is the catch?" he finally asked. Again, Moses Samuel sighed.

"Good question; and you are right of course. The concert will be selling a very exciting product -you. It will also be promoting a cause which is very dear to my heart. With you standing on the platform of our cause, our message will ring for weeks and probably for years all over the world." he replied.

"How much are you offering?" Ex-Man asked, intrigued and amused.

"Two million Pounds for the concert. A quarter million to you even if you decide not to go with me. So how would you vote, brother?"

"I like the money, but why me? For fuck's sake for that kind of money you could go resurrect the fucking Stones again." Ex-Man laughed.

"Another great question. It is because you fit perfectly into our plans - the music is just perfect - blues. Soul, funk, rap; it is a progressive development. Tell me which do you think is the greatest musical era ever? Was it the sixties, seventies or eighties?

"Depends on what sort of music you are talking about."

"Assuming me and you were twins, what would your response be?" Moses Samuel persisted.

"Well, if you put it that way, I would say it was the seventies. This would not be fair on the sixties though because the seventies borrowed a lot from the sixties. Crap began to get into music in the eighties, I think. Yes, I would say seventies." Ex-Man offered Moses Samuel nodded appreciatively

"I have a ten-foot high portrait Of Isaac Hayes on the wall in my office. He is still my idol. I ought to have BB King and Jimi Hendrix on the wall too. I mean, Jimi was boss, man."

"Yes, Jimi was a rarity in his time. Not really my kind of music but Little Wing was really cool. I intend to do my own remix of that one soon."

"I quite love James Brown, Aretha Franklin, Ray Charles and all those guys from Stax. I think I should also have smaller portraits of Stevie Wonder, Tina Turner and of course you can't forget Michael Jackson, Smokey Robinson, and Marvin Gaye. "

"Barry White"

"Yes, him too." Moses Samuel enthusiastically agreed.

"By the time you're done, you may not have any more space left on your wall for even a thumbtack. But I am quite interested to know, how did you find me?" Ex-Man suddenly turned serious.

"When you've got my kind of money and contacts, it may not be so difficult to locate anyone. Let's just leave it at that. Understand however that your identity is completely safe with me.," Moses Samuel assured.

"Fair enough. What is this stuff that I will be promoting?"

"It is not this stuff; it will soon be the most interesting movement and monument in the entire United Kingdom." Moses Samuel assured. From his coat pocket, he brought out a small tablet computer, switched it on to display the simulated picture of an enormous building which looked like a gaudily painted supermarket.

"What the heck is that?" Ex-Man scratched his head, bewildered.

"That is The Psychedelic Shack," Moses Samuel replied.

Moses Samuel nodded silently, eyes glazed.

"You put that up anywhere in England, and it's going to look like a rude finger in the face of civilization, man," Ex-Man exclaimed.

"Maybe that is the point of it," Moses Samuel laughed. "Now my own question, do you like animals?"

"Indifferent. I have never lived long enough with any," Ex-Man shrugged.

"Well, indifferent is a good start," Moses Samuel nodded. And then proceeded to tell Ex-Man the zaniest plan He's ever heard in his life.

The guy was crazy, Ex-Man thought. But crazy or not, Ex-Man walked away from the discussion, with his bank account two hundred and fifty thousand pounds richer – which was more than enough money to buy himself a better transmitter, and to do a lot more. He also left with enough respect for the mad millionaire to buy into Moses Samuel's crazy plan

CHAPTER 10

"I have got a problem" Frank was telling Maureen next evening. Actually, he was telling himself, only that Maureen was there to listen. He was yet trying to recover from last night's rowdy gig: a blur of noise, flashing lights, sweaty bodies, and booze. He had slept all morning and was at this time attempting to make his tender stomach accept some food. Maureen was engrossed with her accounting, but she had looked briefly up, distracted.

"What is the problem Frank?" she asked.

"I am trying to track a stolen item; there is a lot of money involved," Frank told her.

Maureen abandoned her accounting, drew a chair and sat next to him. She rested her chin on his shoulder. Frank found this uncomfortable, especially while trying to eat a reluctant lunch.

"I like the money bit. How much is involved?" Maureen asked, popping a pea in her mouth from Frank's plate.

"You will pay for that," Frank rebuked.

"How much is the reward?" Maureen persisted.

"None of your business" Frank said

"I thought you needed help," Maureen started to leave, looking disappointed.

"Unfortunately, I am not permitted to tell you. That will amount to a breach of professional ethics, you understand? But in any case, this is the situation; some stuff got stolen from a shop somewhere in Eastham, and the owner wants me to find them for him."

"What stuff got stolen?"

"I can't exactly tell you about that either. But they included money, jewelry, and some personal stuff; a lucky charm."

"Eastham, you said?"

"That's right. Not too far from Upton Park. I can't tell you exactly where since that will be a breach of professional ethics." Frank told her like he had said too much already.

"Why don't you go talk with the Snake?" Maureen told him.

"The Snake; is that a who or a what?"

"His real name is Sam Donahue. He runs an auction scam in the High Street circuits around the East End. Straight as a corkscrew he is. But you tell him you are from me. We went to school together. He always has his ears open."

"What sort of school was that, Maureen? No wonder your meals cost a fortune." Frank ribbed her.

"Oh you can afford it; that's all that matters," she said, going back to her bookkeeping.

Frank finished his food, thanked Maureen for the tip and left. He had thought to go up to Stratford to see Sade but changed his mind. He just didn't have the energy for a chat. Instead, he went home, switched on the television to the football channel, turned off the volume and called Sade. They did have a long chat after all.

"You know I actually earned nearly three thousand pounds this week without much sweat," Frank updated her.

"Fantastic! So we're going to be rich then," Sade replied

"Fingers crossed. What have you been up to?" Frank asked.

"I have been busy preparing for the exhibition. The samples have been quite a hit. I am so excited."

"Great! Would you like to come over?" Frank half-heartedly asked.

"No, I am too tired," Sade sighed

●　　　●　　　●　　　●　　　●

Next day was Sunday. Frank resolved to go check Sam the Snake out in the East End. He knew about these auction scams and always wondered how people still got caught by them. The method was simple and like all scams based on greed. What the perpetrators did was post a lot of bills all over the neighborhood announcing an auction and promising mad deal such as a twenty-inch color television for something as ridiculous as fifteen pounds; a camcorder for ten pounds and such. That was how the stage was set.

Most people were actually initially brought by curiosity; they wanted to see if it was actually possible to buy a Rolex watch for six pounds, and surprise, at the initial stage of the heist some people actually did win those goods, only they were part of the heist; wolves hiding amongst the innocent lambs. Then the hustle would quite suddenly change gear. The innocent onlookers are shown the star attractions – typically a giant television priced to go for around ninety pounds, or a top range Bose media center which a lucky person should be able to take home for merely seventy-five pounds. The condition, however, would be that to bid on those you needed to bid first on some smaller knickknack.

Frank had been in such an auction before, and he had lost forty pounds purchasing some worthless shit for five times what they would have cost in the market, hoping to eventually win himself a motorbike priced at one hundred pounds. But near the end of the minor auction, there had been a bit of commotion, the high price props were suddenly disappeared and so were the sweet-tongued auctioneer and his cohorts. The dumbfounded victims were left behind, sheepishly looking one another in the face; ashamed of their own greed and how it had brought those to this sorry pass. Some would wail having lost their entire savings and rent in the scam. Somehow though the police tolerated the game and so it persisted.

●　　●　　●　　●　　●

Frank decided to begin his hunt at Ilford and then move southward doing Barking, Eastham, in that order. He took the train from Hackney and alighted at Ilford. As he exited the station his eyes were arrested by a Pakistani couple waiting outside to catch a bus. They seemed well into their fifties. The portly woman had a red dot painted on her forehead and a sour expression on her face. The man looked quite glum, much gloomier than his grey suit. But Frank was really not interested in either of them. He was more interested in the pendant hanging from the woman's neck, trying to decide if it was Raj's stolen luckily charm. This certainly looked more like a golden banana. Why anyone would want to hang a banana from around their neck, he wondered? The woman smiled back at him.

"Why is that man looking at you?" the old Pakistani mentioned to his wife.

"He is looking at me?" The wife asked, smiling more fiercely.

"Yes, he certainly was looking at you. Why is he looking at you like that? You are not even beautiful."

"Well, he is looking at me"; she sucked air through her teeth.

"He must be a sex maniac," the man was convinced. Hand clenched behind his back, he resolutely walked up to Frank.

"Put your eyes away. Stop looking at her - my wife," he rebuked.

Frank was surprised and quite embarrassed that he had been staring. He muttered an apology. The bus thankfully came at last, and the grinning Pakistani woman gave him a dainty wave.

"Bye bye sex maniac," she said.

•　　　•　　　•　　　•　　　•

It was never really difficult to find one of the bogus High Street auctions. You only needed to follow the trail of crude posters. Sam was not on High Street, Ilford; not in Barking either which was merely ten minutes away. Frank, however, struck gold at Eastham where he caught Sam fleeing another abruptly terminated auction. Sam looked exactly like Maureen had described him: Elvis sideburns, flowered shirt, and nearly Italian features. Frank caught up with him as he was about to enter his Ford Escort.

"What you want? I warned you people not to spend your rent, didn't I? There is no refund; I don't even have your money," he growled at Frank.

"I am not from the auction, Maureen Mahoney sent me," Frank assured him.

Sam looked apprehensive for a moment them motioned with his head for Frank to get in the car; driving quickly away from the hostile customers emerging from the empty shop, which was under renovation, and where the scam auction had taken place.

They stopped at a noodle restaurant on Barking Road. Frank was hungry; he ordered the house special fried rice with carrot juice. Sam had noodle soup.

"What did you want to see me about," Sam eventually asked. And so Frank told him about the robbery at Raj's shop, and especially the method - which he added, he had also witnessed while in a bank a few weeks back. Sam was genuinely amused.

"So what do you want me to do? You are out of luck though; I didn't do it."

"Of course, you didn't. I would never have thought that you did. Maureen only said you always had your ears to the ground."

"Maureen ... Maureen ...that girl, will always misunderstand me. I am not a criminal, I am a businessman."

"I am sure. Of course, you are not a criminal; that's why you are here and not in prison," Frank agreed.

Sam shrugged. "Anyway I will keep my ears open for you and also ask some of the blokes work for me if they see anything."

Frank gave Same Donahue his card, after finishing his meal, and left the noodle restaurant. He had a date with Sade, and so he took the train for Stratford.

● ● ● ● ●

Frank went with Sade to see a film at the Stratford Picturehouse, and then to McDonald"s for ice cream. Returning home later in the night, he was not aware of a man who followed at a discrete distance behind him. His name was Abu, a small thin Pakistan; and he kept trying to muffle his frequent sneezes with an already wet handkerchief.

CHAPTER 11

Most of the next day had been spent in a drudge. Not knowing where next to pick up the trail from, Frank spent the day window shopping around Ilford and prowling the Upton Park market in the faint hope that a solution would suddenly leap into sight; but he had no such luck.

Trevor called around six in the evening and asked Frank to come over. Trevor had just moved into a new flat in Canary Wharf. It was a large spacious place which he had sparsely but very tastefully decorated in wood, soft leathers, and plush carpeting. Trevor was really moving up in the world, and again Frank wondered where all this money was coming from. Trevor's girlfriend, Sandy, a very pretty Dominican girl, was just leaving when Frank arrived. She gave Frank a quick hug and was gone. Sandy was a very talented sound engineer, who had worked with several music concert organizers.

Together they went to a pub down the road, where they bought pizza. Trevor ordered Caliber beer which Frank detested, grimacing with every sip and wondering why anyone in their right mind would want to drink non-alcoholic beer. This definitely wasn't beer; it ought to be properly labeled medicine, Frank gave his honest opinion

"Take a look at this "; Trevor gave him a small handbill. Frank had seen it before, almost everywhere as a fact including on television. It was about the Retro Renaissance concert - the Ex-Man's premiere concert coming up at the O2.

"I have seen that before; what about it?" Frank asked Trevor.

"What about it is that we are going to be in that show. We will in the opening acts."

Frank was genuinely bowled. "Fantastic. How did you swing that?"

"Oh well, I have ways. Actually Sandy is also in the organizing. She sort of suggested that we be in it. Mad Scientist duels with MC Wire at the O2."

"Absolutely fantastic, Trevor. Fucking unbelievable," Frank was absolutely thrilled.

"I thought you would say something like that. Just imagine, it's going to be the big night at the O2. Everyone from London and all over have come over to see the show of the year: where the sensational Ex-Man finally reveals himself. Only he doesn't quite do that yet for an hour or so after the stage opens. First comes a lineup of other acts - Seal opens first, next comes Sade Adu, George Benson and a host of other stars, and of course MC Wire and The Mad Scientist to add a lot more variety. And finally a puff of smoke I think, and out emerges Ex-Man; only that we don't get to leave the stage for a while, we will be there with the Ex-Man. And the eyes of the entire world will be on us Frank." '

"Un-fucking believable."

"Never mind, just enjoy. If you and me had to know, then there goes the mystery behind Ex-Man, right. Just enjoy that it was Sandy who sort of wrote us unto the script."

This was all too much for Frank to take. He dumped his Caliber and went to get himself a real beer.

•　　•　　•　　•　　•

Frank found Sade at Mile End station where she had been waiting for him. Frank was so excited he couldn't wait to tell her the good news, and he'd called her; only she'd been shopping in West End at the time and promised to meet up with Frank at the station. They took a bus for Hackney together. On the bus, Frank told her everything he'd heard from Trevor.

"That's unbelievable," Sade was sincerely pleased for them. "How did Trevor, get that done."

"Well, actually Sandy did the magic. Seems well connected and it's like she's in charge of the sound for the Ex-Man concert, and so That's probably how she could fix us up."

"Trevor seems to be living quite up there these days, don't you think? First a thirty thousand quid BMW and now He's rubbing shoulder with top cream. Something exciting in definite happening in his life," Sade observed.

"Yes I did think Trevor was selling stuff, but he is not the type. He's just a hard-working music producer."

Frank had known Trevor since they were in school together at London Metropolitan College four years back. Their gigs had started as a lark which would have been considered over when they left school and drifted apart. But it had again resumed about a year back when Trevor called him up one day, to tell him he was in search of a tandem DJ act to complement his event promotion business. Frank at this present time found himself wondering what it would take to be as moderately successful in the event promotion thing business as Trevor had been, but he gave up the idea. He wasn't any good at organizing anything at all.

They picked up a chicken dinner at a KFC, and since it was an unusually warm night, Sade decided to walk along with Frank to his place. Frank thought for them to sit on the steps leading up to the house and eat their take out, but Sade thought differently. She wanted to watch X-factor which was just about to start.

A rolled-up notepaper was found hanging from the door keyhole. Frank took it out, and without reading opened the door and let Sade in. He dumped the note in the trash basket with the rest of the junk mail. But to Sade, the note didn't look like any other junk mail. Nobody sent junk mail with pink perfumed notepaper, so she'd picked it out of the trash.

"It says, Frank, call me please. xxx .Nancy. Look like it's a message for you" Sade gave him the letter.

"Nancy. How did she know where I live?" Frank frowned at the note.

"You know her then? "Sade rolled her eyes.

"I did; I haven't seen her for more than three years though. No, That's not quite right; I saw her a few months ago at a gig. We used to live together, but we broke up. She wanted to marry me. And then she started shagging my friend because I didn't want to know."

"Looks like you are now the friend she wants to shag next on the side the way I see it," Sade wickedly told him.

"That's all over. In fact, sHe's called my phone several times since I met her at the party and I didn't call her back. I wonder how she knew where I live."

"That's the funniest thing I've heard. Are you not on the voters" register?" Sade told him as she flopped into the sofa and switched on the television in time is to catch a sadistic judge telling another distressed competitor who's on his knees begging to be given a second chance. The only future he could see for the destroyed young fellow on his knees was a permanent job, working in a Timberland clothing store as a cleaner; definitely not as the next Justin Timberlake., the judge assured without mercy.

"What a pompous disgusting asshole," Sade was sufficiently irked.

"Yes, he is, but he makes a lot of money being a pompous disgusting asshole. And when you have got a lot of money, you can afford to be an asshole and not give a damn what anyone thinks."

"So, what you going to do about your old flame; that just came back into your life then?" Sade asked, not quite yet off the topic.

"Nothing, I'd just ignore her."

"She knows where you live. She thinks you important enough to trace you up."

"Never mind about Nancy. She will go away," Frank tried to assure her. But Sade didn't seem convinced. Frank took her off the topic and told her about Raj and Sam the Snake up in Eastham.

"This is not a newspaper job thing anymore you realize, you are dealing with real criminals, and they do sound dangerous," Sade warned him to be careful.

The X-Factor show ended with another fat, forty-ish woman contestant making a brave declaration: "I am good; nothing you say to me can change that. I am good, and next time you see me, you will have to fork out a lot of money. You people can't judge a pissing contest in a bloody pub," she scolded and off the stage she went in a huff.

Frank saw Sade to the train station and returned home, picking up some beer from a grocery shop on the way. In the street, a lone figure shuffled past the house. Abu walked past the house several times - up the street and back again. After about an hour, he slouched off blowing noisily into his wet handkerchief - his head buried deep in the upturned collar of his coat.

CHAPTER 12

A gig in Hell.

Frank had been having a nightmare. There he was alone at a gig without Trevor, which didn't make any sense, but then dreams rarely made any sense. One million watts of manic music surged and pulsed from the glowing hot walls all around him. Swarthy demons stomped noisily all across the dance floor and swung dangerously from entrails dripping with blood and hanging from the sooty ceiling like thick vines from trees in a jungle. The air in that cavernous hall smelled of smoke, spirits and burning sulfur. Debonair angels peered inquisitively from lofty heights, their shimmering white robes blemished by the flickering strobe lights from inside the cavern. Funky demons were doing endless backslides to a Shalamar song.

This night you won't forget
Gonna make this a night to remember
"Cause your love I won't regret
Gonna make this a night

Trolls vomited excitedly over one another in competition. This night certainly had the promise of being remembered for all eternity. But suddenly the music had stopped; and no matter what Frank tried, he hadn't been able to get the equipment to function anymore. Tens of thousands of evil faces turned toward him. Long daggers, sabers, heavy caliber pistols, machine guns, garrotes, nail pullers, nutcrackers, eye gougers and sundry instruments of torture were being produced. Frank could feel the temperature rising all around – long tongues of flames billowed from cavernous gashes in the crimson walls and floors. Enormous bolts of lightning crisscrossed the black high ceilings. Thunder shook the evil temple like monstrous earthquake tremors.

A drop of beer to cool my tongue Father Abraham, he silently, desperately prayed; his head pulsing painfully as he cowered behind his dead equipment, awaiting an excruciating death.

The angry horde was soon upon him. It was Spencer Cowley who reached Frank first, his malevolent grin revealing sharp teeth which dribbled blood. In his huge hairy hand, Spencer Cowley held a flaming dagger.

Where was Trevor? Frank despaired; one could never anymore depend on a friend to stick around when trouble came.

"Deadmeat*!!*" Spencer bellowed as he went for Frank's throat with the dagger. And all the bells of hell rang with a dreadful din.

•   •   •   •   •

It was Frank's ringing phone that woke him up the next morning from this nightmare. The time looked around eight, but it seemed to him like he had slept for only a couple of hours.

"Oi; is that Frankie?" It was a voice of someone Frank knew he ought to remember but for several seconds was unable to put a face to it. Gradually it came to him. Damn, he'd completely forgotten about Harvey Simpson.

"How are you Harvey?" Frank replied. But Harvey didn't seem in the mood to be pleasant.

"Where is my wife?" He asked.

"I was thinking of coming to see you later today with my report, "Frank told him.

"Never mind the freakin" report, where is Ida?"

"I haven't seen her today, isn't she with you?" Frank tried to maneuver.

"If she was with me, I wouldn't be calling you, would I? You was supposed to keep an eye on her. She Hasn't been home for two nights. I paid you for this, you dickhead; where is my wife?"

"Don't call me names, Harvey," Frank protested; but Harvey wasn't finished yet.

"She's not home tonight, and you can't tell me where she is, I'm going to kill you," Harvey said, clicking off. Frank called Harvey's phone, immensely confused, but he didn't answer.

Now, where could Ida Simpson be? Frank wondered. There was only one place he could think of. So, later in the morning, he took the bus to Dagenham. There was no point hanging out at the train station this time, so he headed for Jimmy's house careful not to approach it from the usual direction. Indeed Frank did not approach it at all, fearing another encounter with the skinheads. There was a field about two hundred yards away. There, Frank sat on a bench from which he could get a good view of Jimmy's door, as usual pretending to read a newspaper. But nothing happened at that door even though he sat in the bench till five in the evening.

It thereafter struck him that he had no reason to be doing any clandestine surveillance. Heck, Ida was his client too, even a better paying client than Harvey All he had to do was go up to the door and talk to her if she was there. So Frank went to Jimmy's door and knocked. No response. He knocked several times, and it actually appeared like the house was empty. He had wasted an entire day sitting on a bench, and he felt angry with himself.

Frank went up to Trevor place on Canary Wharf. Trevor showed him round the flat, to Frank's genuine amazement at the snazzy decor. Finally, they stopped in a huge room that had been converted into a recording studio filled with equipment, many of which Frank couldn't even identify.

"Sandy fixed this place for me. She got a Japanese bloke to work with her on this. I've also got serious plans you know. I've been always thinking why not bring some young talent in once a while and try to make some money off them. You know the way Branson ripped off a lot of young blood with his Virgin label,'" Trevor proudly told him. "

"Well Branson also created some big names, didn't he?" Frank reminded Trevor."

"That's my vision man; to create big names" Trevor seriously nodded.

"You've been doing a lot of Ex-Man remixes for our gigs I notice, Trevor," Frank said.

"That should account for the reason why Sandy didn't find it too difficult to get us in the concert, I am sure." Trevor laughed.

The doorbell and Trevor opened to let in a geeky kid.

"Frank, this is Wu-Tan; he fixed my studio. Wu-Tan is studying electronics at Imperial College and has been developing some sort of tracking device which he thinks should make him a fortune back home." Trevor introduced the kid.

Wu-Tan nodded his smile distant. He sat behind the studio console, clapped a headphone over his ears and fiddled with knobs, switches, and slides before him. Finally, he laid down the headphones.

"This your tracking device invention; how does it work, Wu-Tan?" Frank asked.

"Doesn't work yet, but soon will. Same technology as tracking a phone really but more precise and the devices are smaller." Wu-Tan replied.

"Just what I need. Then, I'd just need to sit at home and track anyone while watching TV. The hard part of it I guess would be how to get the person I am tracking to wear the device" Frank laughed

"You are right, of course. It will probably be illegal in some countries too," Wu-Tan agreed with him.

•   •   •   •   •

It was after ten when Frank approached home. The three skinheads sitting at the steps told him something was not quite right. They rose as Frank approached them. He could smell the cheap cider they were drinking from twenty feet away. Frank initially thought they looked like Patchy and the blokes from Jimmy's neighborhood at Dagenham, but he soon realized these ones were bigger, not that they looked any friendlier.

There were several possibilities, Frank thought. They could be the Dagenham pack, and they'd seen him prowling around earlier in the day. They were probably not even Jimmy's team, but some other monsters sent by Harvey to exercise his treat. Again, they were probably just some sociopathic white guys looking to kick someone's ass just for the fun of it tonight. In any case, Frank was not going to ask them. He fled down the way he'd come, and could hear heavy boots coming along behind him. A couple of bottles exploded around him as he ran, and he ran even harder. He bolted toward Homerton Road and was lucky to find a bus going toward Stratford, into which he gratefully threw himself, before it moved on from the bus stop.

•   •   •   •   •

"This detective thing doesn't seem to be going very well, is it?" Sade was quite anxious, after, she'd heard Frank out.

"What isn't? For all I know, they could be just some bloody drunk idiots going crazy tonight," Frank pretended not to understand.

"If you say so. But why don't you get a safe job, Frank? You will probably be able to find some temporary work with the council until another newspaper job comes in." Sade certainly was very worried.

"Ok, I will give your advice a shot. I will go looking around tomorrow," Frank told her, not intending to do any such thing. All he could think of was the ten thousand pounds Raj was going to pay him, which was nearly half what he could hope to earn, working full time for a whole year on a bloody council job.

Additionally, he had a plan to eventually get back into journalism, and the case he was working on he felt sure would be the negotiating ticket. Frank had sent a story proposal to the editor of The Times. *The Great East End Heist*, the story proposal had read. Frank had written to ask if they would like to see the story of the great heist at East London, and the editor had said yes. The skeleton of the story Frank had in his computer. Raj's case would enable him to add flesh to it; and when the story finally hits the street, with the by-line of Frank O'Dwyer, even Spencer Cowley would regret firing him. And thereafter, Frank O'Dwyer could be able to write his own employment letter for any newspaper in the country. Heck, he could also make a little fortune from a book too. *The Great East End Heist.*

CHAPTER 13

Frank left Sade's flat in the morning before she woke up. Hoping that the skinheads hanging around his place were night creatures, he headed for home.

They had gone. Nevertheless, for a few minutes, Frank stood on the steps leading up into the house and looked up and down the street several times before feeling safe enough to enter the house. Again, he did a double check before opening the door to the flat. Still nothing out of place out there. On the floor, he found a sheet of paper which had been stuffed through the letter hole with the rest of the junk literature. It stood out because it was actually grease paper, the type you got your fish and chips wrapped in. "*EDIOT*" was scrawled on the back of the sheet in blue felt-tip pen. When he unfolded the sheet, he read:

I no were u live, ediot

Frank crumpled the sheet and binned it. Who was it this time? First, it was Nancy from the past and now some asshole from wherever. On second thought he took the sheet from the bin, and folded it into his pocket, feeling very angry.

Frank called Harvey Simpson's, phone. He answered this time and sounded quite drunk, even though it was barely eight in the morning. This man really had problems, Frank noted. Nevertheless, he made an appointment to see Harvey later in the morning at the Funky Munky. Harvey said eleven would be okay.

Frank found him faithfully waiting at the Funky Munky, in exactly the same he sat the last time Frank was here. He even felt sure that Harvey had exactly the same quantity of beer in his mug. Someone could possibly do a timeless portrait on this man, Frank thought.

"Where is Ida?" Harvey asked in a tired voice.

"Harvey, if you don't know where your wife is, neither do I. I mean she's your wife, not mine," Frank tried to reason this out with him, but Harvey Simpson didn't look like he wanted to be reasonable.

"I paid you to follow her," he sighed.

"Yes, I tried to follow her, but she keeps disappearing. I think she might be training to be a magician," Frank said without humor.

Frank had visited the bank earlier. He took three fifty pound notes from his pocket and slapped the notes on the table.

"Here is your money back; I don't want to do this anyone," He told Harvey.

But Harvey only shook his head slowly and morosely.

"I paid you to follow Ida "; he persisted.

"I quit this case so kindly tell your punks to stop harassing me, okay?" Frank told him. Harvey seemed confused for a moment.

"You've got some punks harassing you, you said?"

"Yes, three chimps who think they can scare me; but they have got another think coming. Now call them off me, or there will be hell to pay. I will call the police," Frank warned. Harvey Simpson took his money and tucked the notes in his pocket. A mad smile played on his tired face.

"Those were not my punks. Those ones I don't know about. My own punks may come visiting later, and they are not afraid of the police," he chuckled.

That took the air out of Frank for a minute. Seeing no point in carrying the argument any further, however, he left the Funky Munky.

"*My own punks may come visiting later,*" Harvey had said. Now if those people had not been from Harvey and not likely from Ida, who were they? Had they been sent by Raj? Not likely; he had Raj's two thousand. Had they been sent by Nancy to beat him up for ignoring her? Possible, but Nancy hated skinheads, though the situation could have changed over the years. You never knew with women.

●　　●　　●　　●　　●

Following Sade's suggestion, he called some borough offices to inquire about job vacancies. Hackney was perpetually engaged. Newham Borough phone was picked up by an operator:

"Good morning, this is the help desk of London Borough of Newham..." the Asian girl began.

"Who can I speak to about job vacancies?" Frank cut her short.

"Kindly let me do my job and finish before you say anything," she rebuked.

"Ok sorry," Frank told her; not at all sorry. Pacified, the operator again launched into her script:

"Good morning, this is the help desk of London Borough of Newham. Our opening hours is from nine-o-clock to five-o-clock. If you know the extension of the department you want, please dial it now otherwise how may I help you?" she heartily responded.

Frank decided instead to hang up.

CHAPTER 14

"Hey Sam, you've got anything for me yet?"

"Who are you? "Sam suspicious answered; obviously, he didn't have Frank in his phone directory.

"It's me Sam, Frank from Maureen. I spoke with you the other day; remember me? About all those goings-on in the neighborhood; shops getting knocked off and all."

"Oh, that Frank," recognition came to Sam. "Been meaning to call you, but I sort of lost your number. Could we meet in about an hour? Say, do you know Valentines Park?"

Frank said he knew Valentine's Park, and yes he would meet Sam there as promised. Valentine's Park was just midway between Ilford and Gants Hill, and he reckoned it should take no more than thirty minutes by bus, from Whitechapel Station.

Intuition warned him that things were not quite right. The feeling drew his attention to a man who seemed to be looking into a shop window but really wasn't. He was looking into the shop window to avoid meeting someone's eyes - in this case, Frank's eyes. The fellow seemed to be doing exactly what the detective course prescribed for when you were following someone, and you seemed in danger of being discovered – keep staring into a shop window.

Something told Frank that he'd been in contact with this guy several times over the past few days. It was the guy's bad cold that gave him away. This morning it was the sneezing that made Frank remember him. He had initially thought this was nothing unusual. There would probably be dozens of Pakistanis in London with a bad cold, and there was no point getting paranoid. Nevertheless, on a hunch, Frank crossed the road and decided to take a bus towards the Tower of London instead - in an opposite direction from Ilford. His hunch was rewarded as the man also crossed over and got on the bus behind him He did it quite gracefully too, and Frank agreed with himself that he may have a lot to learn from this fellow about covert surveillance. Pity about his flu though.

From the bus stop, Frank walked down Minories toward the Tower Hill station, taking a quick glance back and satisfied to find the Pakistani guy about twenty-five yards behind him. Frank headed past the tube station toward Trinity Square Gardens and there merged himself into a group of tourists gazing lazily at the Tower of London which stood about a hundred yards away across the road.

Two policemen strolling by gave him a better idea than running. Frank headed straight for his follower. As the Eagle training course suggested, if you were tailing a person and then the subject turned around, don't panic or make abrupt movements; act naturally and maybe even walk past your subject. This person who had been following him was definitely one cool guy because he obeyed all the instruction to the letter. He just appeared to look through Frank and would have walked right past even as Frank turned and approached him, not about to give him an easy way out.

"Why are you following me?" Frank shouted at him; quite satisfied to find him unnerved by all the eyes that had suddenly turned in his direction. Next Frank headed for the two policemen, pointing at his hapless pursuer.

"This man has been following me. He's threatened to kill me. Save me from him," Frank appealed to the two policemen.

The police were momentarily confused and then amazed, then all duty. As expected they called Abu aside. From his scuffed shoes and worn coat, which seemed to be his disguise, he looked very much out of place in Central London at this time of the day. So out of place that he could very well have just worn a huge badge all over his chest, that said "illegal immigrant." Wrong disguise for the wrong place, perhaps. In any case, he looked distrustful enough for the police to take more than ordinary interest in his mission, giving Frank sufficient time to slip away into the tube station and catch an eastward bound train.

Sam was already waiting at Valentines Park when Frank got there. Frank found him sitting on a bench overlooking the bird lake, smoking a cigarette. He offered Frank a cigarette and Frank declined.

"You got some lead for me?" Frank asked him. But Sam was in no hurry. He led Frank off first to get some ice cream and sandwiches from the park café.

"Have you ever heard of the Barefoot Revolution?" Sam asked when they returned to the lake.

"No I haven't. What is that about?" Frank asked him.

"Sounds really wacky, doesn't it? Some nutty scheme with the aim to make everyone in the world do without shoes because shoes are a product of cruelty to animals" Sam laughed. "

"That's crazy; most shoes today are entirely made from synthetic stuff," Frank also laughed.

"Yeah; I am sure they know that. Apparently, they just think that it will be a symbolic gesture of oneness with nature since animals don't wear shoes," Sam chuckled as he gulped his ice cream. Frank couldn't also help but laugh.

"That's absolutely bat-shit: so what has this got to do with my problem Sam?"

"Nothing," Sam said, and Frank was surprised.

"So why did you bring it up then?"

"Because, well it sounded so crazy to me too and I thought I ought to share it with somebody. Isn't it the craziest thing you've ever heard Frankie? Fucking crazy." Frank wondered if Sam might be on drugs. He did at that moment look the type.

"So what update do you have on what we discussed earlier, Sam?"

"Oh, that? I am afraid I don't have anything presently. I promise to keep my ear to the ground nevertheless," he said quite pensively.

Frank left convinced that Sam was doing drugs.

CHAPTER 15

Frank found Raj near the door of his shop, hands clasped pensively behind his back and fretfully pacing across the front; completely oblivious of the traffic all around him. Raj's face lit up when he saw Frank.

"Ah, Mister Detective ...come...come"; he ushered Frank through the busy shop and into the back office.

"Did you find anything for me yet?"

"Not yet, unfortunately, but I am looking. I do have some serious leads though. The robbers seem to live right here in East London, and it's just a matter of time till I fish them out," Frank lied.

"Good...good. I thought they live in East London too; horrible idiots. Thank you for finding them. I do not know what I will do if I do not find my lucky charm. My life and children's life will be destroyed for many generations."

"Come on, you are exaggerating. Why do you say that? I don't believe people still hold on to these sort of superstitious shit," Frank told him.

"Don't be so crude with your mouth. This is not superstitious shit, as you say; this is a lucky charm," Raj waved an angry finger in his face.

"Now don't get your balls in an uproar Raj; I was just making one of my usual stupid comments," Frank pleaded.

"Yes most certainly; it is your stupid comment. And for your information I do not have any ball to put in an uproar; or whatever you call it," Raj was not easily pacified. Frank changed the topic.

"Now why do you think this lucky charm is absolutely important to your future, Raj? It could be just a hoax."

"I do not think, Mister Detective; It is the fact. The Crooked Bullet was created for my great, great grandfather in Bangalore. It is to be passed to the first male child as soon as he gets married to ensure that it protects everyone down the generations. The curse : if it is not passed on ,the luck does not flow again, it just stops."

"Hmm...That is interesting. So how do you make the luck flow? You rub it like a magic lamp every morning. Or I'd rather say a magic dick?" Frank was genuinely intrigued.

"I do not rub a magic dick in the morning, you silly man." Are you sure you are a detective? "Raj fumed. Frank held up his hands in a pleading gesture.

"Why are you having me followed, Raj?" Frank decided to shoot him a surprise question; glad to see Raj completely amazed.

"Why am I having you followed?" Raj shrugged his shoulder.

"Well, a group of lunatics chased me up the street couple of night ago, with broken bottles. This morning a wet-nosed fellow followed me all around town for hours. Someone must have sent them after me, and I just can't figure this one out yet. I was hoping you'll be able to help me out."

"I am sorry I don't know who is chasing you Mister Detective. I mean you are the detective; I am only a shop keeper. Your work is to find people, no?"

"Never mind; I believe you. About your missing properties I will soon get to the bottom of this dirty business no matter whose ox is gored" Frank sighed, turning to leave the room. He was surprised to again find Raj in a new rage.

"You do not have to find out whose ox is God. My ox is God. All I want you to do is find my lucky charm, you silly man."

Frank gave him thumbs-up and left.

Outside, he thought he saw his erstwhile pursuer, Abu, hastily dodging into the market. He decided to follow pretending to be a shopper while he kept his eyes roving around. He nevertheless bought a bag of kiwi fruit for a pound as well as a bag of shiny black plums, wondering how hard a life these merchants must be living to sell so cheap. He soon found himself in front of a meat shop where a bellicose Ethiopian meat cutter was having a spirited argument with an equal enraged Somali. A few other customers watched in amusement; obviously, scenes like this were common.

"No...no...no," the Somali was saying, emphatically punching the air with his finger. "This is small chicken; I want big chicken. I keep telling you this every day; you never listen to me."

"Of course, I am listening to you, only you do not understand what you are saying," the Ethiopian seemed not in a good mood either.

"Okay, you are listening to me. Why then every day you give me small chicken?"

"Because big chicken is big money you idiot."

A flurry of unintelligible gibberish followed from both sides, and a fist fight seemed imminent. Frank was surprised to see both suddenly collapse into laughter; the crowd dispersed in embarrassment. This did not look like sane territory at all. Frank found that the man he had been following was not his pursuer. He left the market and called Maureen.

"Is Sam Donahue on drugs?" he blurted out.

"Why do you say that?" Maureen sounded very puzzled.

"Well, he dragged me halfway across town to tell me a story That's full of bullshit. Really pissed off with that guy I am."

"Well, Sam is a little funny, but I am sure He's not on drugs; not in any heavy way at least. He doesn't have the head for such things," Maureen was quite firm.

"Okay, I believe you. Have you seen some funny guys, hanging around lately? I mean funny guys with low cut hair and who don't seem to have anything to do but wander?" Frank anxiously inquired; not wanting to be surprised by a deadly gang waiting for him at the Hard Luck Cafe. He could hear Maureen laughing uneasily.

"This is London, Frank. There are funny guys with low cut hair and heavy boots, who don't seem to have anything to do, all over the place. Are you sure you're okay?"

"Never mind, Maureen. Forget I asked. See you in a couple of hours. I assure you I am okay." he felt embarrassed that it was now him who seemed to be on drugs.

CHAPTER 16

Raj sounded extremely distressed when he called Frank again next morning. Frank found Raj pacing the front of the shop as usual while a small shiny-faced Indian guy who looked very distraught watched. Back in the office, Raj handed Frank a sheet of paper. Frank read what was written on it.

"It looks like a ransom letter," he said to Raj.

"Of course, I know it is a ransom letter. Somebody has pinched my daughter. Everywhere in this country they pinch something. First, they pinch my jewelry and my money, they pinch my lucky charm, and now they pinch my daughter," Raj was impossibly both angry and distressed at the same time.

"They are asking for two hundred thousand. They must be insane, nobody is worth that much"; Frank gave his honest impression.

"My Rupinder is worth that and more. My Rupinder is worth her weight in gold," the young fellow spoke for the first time; his voice squeaky and timid.

"This is Kalyan Shetty; he is my future son-in-law; and now that his bride is pinched, he has no bride even though the marriage is about two months away. He has no bride, I have no daughter to marry to him." Raj introduced the other Indian guy.

"Come on Raj, this is England, not some fucking banana country. People don't get pinched in England," Frank reasoned.

"In India, they did not pinch my daughter; in England, they pinch" Raj was adamant.

"Okay, so you are going to pay those guys two hundred thousand, right? And then your daughter walks in a week later having gone to spend a week in the Riviera with her lover. And you find that you've just paid two hundred to some prankster. Where do you find that amount of money anyway?" Frank sighed.

"My daughter Rupinder does not go to the Riviera or whatever you call it with a lover; she is to be married to Kalyan here. And for your information, it is not your business to ask me where I get the money to pay" Raj was, as usual, getting angrier by the minute.

"Okay Raj, don't get your balls in an uproar," Frank tried to bring the discussion to normal.

"Again I tell you I don't have any ball in uproar, you silly man"; Raj raved.

"Okay Raj; relax we will get to the bottom of this"

"I am relaxed," Raj was recalcitrant.

"Okay, relax a lot more. So you have resolved to pay these...umh...kidnappers, then?"

"I have no choice do I?"

"But they have not yet given instruction on how to pay, and I believe that will never come, because I still think all this is a hoax." Frank was confident.

"They telephoned me. They want someone to deliver the money in a briefcase, but they have not told me where or when; only to get the money ready. I want you to deliver the money and get my daughter back."

"Why me?" Frank was surprised.

"Because you are a good man for such a thing. I can be sure that it will be done effectively because you are a professional detective." Raj told him. Frank could not help laughing.

"Do you know what kidnappers do to a person who delivers the ransom?" he asked

"I do not know; my daughter is being kidnapped for the first time." Raj truthfully replied

"Well, the fact of life is that in real kidnap cases, neither the person who delivers the money or the kidnapped person ever comes back again." Frank grimly advised.

"They cannot do such a thing to me; this in England," Raj's protested. Kalyan whimpered. Frank spread his hands in submission.

"Nevertheless, I will do what you wish as you said. But it is going to cost you fifteen thousand, seeing that I will be putting my life at risk." Frank told Raj.

You thief! Raj seemed about to say but changed his mind

"I will pay you whatever you want; I just want you to bring my daughter back to me," he said instead. Frank left the small, stuffy office and hasted away through the large crowded shop and into the street. Top on his mind was the resolve to get rid of this case for good.

"Sam Donahue had an accident," Maureen told Frank at the Hard Luck Café; where Frank later went for lunch.

"What happened to him?" Frank wanted to know.

"Seems like he was attacked in an ambush last night and a few things got broken. He's in hospitals right now as I speak."

This was really bad news to Frank. Sam's importance to him had gone beyond the wish to find the people who robbed Raj's shop. Without Sam, the story he had promised The Times might never get finished and there would go his future plans.

In the evening, he took a train to Becontree together with Maureen and walked up to King George's Hospitals to see Sam Donahue. Sam was out of emergency now but had been very cleverly wrapped up in the corner of a ward. His legs and arms were in a plaster cast and suspended from an overhead frame; his jaws were wired shut. Sam's eyes looked extremely pitiable. Frank decided not to ask him any question; there was no point. He shivered with fear though, thinking if they could do this to Sam who was just harmlessly nosing around, they could do a lot worse when they caught up with him; whoever they were.

On the nearby bed, a thoroughly confused old man was being fussed over by a couple of nurses, trying to get him to lie down.

"Why are you all being so nice to me? Where am I?" he kept asking.

"Just lie down Mr. Brown; we'll get you comfortable in a moment," the African nurse was being quite persuasive. But Mr. Brown wasn't having any of that.

"Who are you, people? Why are you being nice to me? Are you the devil? Am I in hell?" he desperately sought to know.

•   •   •   •   •

Frank decided to visit Sade's exhibition at the Barbican Centre. Sade led two models to exhibit her African prints designs to a group of onlookers at her stand. Frank applauded along with the onlookers. It eventually got overwhelming for Frank; there wasn't anything here for him. He hugged Sade before leaving.

•   •   •   •   •

Frank didn't return home till near eight in the night, and as usual, he did not approach the house till he was sure that it was safe to do so. He opened the door to his flat with so much confidence that he was safe. The alarm didn't register until he was in: he realized that he had not needed a key to open the door. But then it was too late to turn back. He found the sitting room in shambles. Whoever had broken into his flat seemed to have an idea what they were supposed to be looking for, but not where to find it. The furniture was scattered, and the cushions slashed. His CDs, stereo and television, were intact though, and nothing seemed to have been stolen as far as he could immediately see.

There was an odor in the air too. Whoever it was that had broken in had definitely left a lot of musk behind. But he found too late that the hunter was still very much about; as a hard object came crashing on his head.

CHAPTER 17

Frank slowly picked himself up and examined his head for blood or bumps. Neither was visible, but he suspected the bump would come later. His assailant had escaped away, but the weapon lay shattered on the floor beside him. It was a heavy porcelain voice with oriental paintings on its side, and which he had inherited from the previous occupant of the flat. Frank had meant to throw it away for months only that Sade liked it, so to him, it hadn't been such a huge loss. The vase now lay scattered in little shards on the floor. Again he examined his head for damage; his finger was now rewarded with a rising bump, but he surely wasn't in danger of dying.

Another look around told him that the slashed chairs were not the only things that he needed to grieve about. His desk was in complete disarray, and his notebook computer was gone. So were all his notes. The computer was old, but it contained all his new and older work samples which were completely irreplaceable. More importantly, though the *East End Heist* story was gone, both his written notes and the computer notes. Not that it bothered him a lot. Most of that story he could recreate quite easily. He was more concerned that these notes had apparently been the target of the person who had raided his flat, and the discovery clearly underlined the danger he was in.

Trevor's call rescued him from his dark thoughts.

"What's with you man?" Trevor said to him

"Not much happening Trevor; only my flat got burgled."

"Jeez, That's terrible; what did they take?" Trevor was genuinely concerned.

"My computer" Frank told him, leaving out the bit about the notes.

"That old crap? The guy must really be desperate for his crack money. You didn't get hurt did you?"

"Just nearly got nutted with a vase. I will survive I am sure," Frank

"Of course, you will, sorry about all that. Are you in the mood to talk about the Ex-Man gig?"

"Why not? Go ahead, man. I mean, are we having like rehearsals? I hear these shows are heavily rehearsed.1, Frank replied.

"Okay, this is how it is. The stage is the group to be laid out like it's Soul Train, yeah? And you know who they have lined up to open?"

"No I don't," Frank miserably told him.

"Okay, you don't. The opening line up will now also include George Benson, Lionel Ritchie, Seal, and Sade. Not your Sade of course. Then we have the stage for a full thirty minutes. Imagine it, Frank, all eyes focused on you for thirty freaking minutes, and after which the Ex-Man explodes onto the stage. Frank! We are going to be famous, man!"

Despite his headache, Frank found his mood lifted at the news.

"Sounds fantastic Trevor what would I be expected to do before? I mean, are we having like rehearsals? I hear these shows are heavily rehearsed."

"That is the beauty of this for us Frank; Sandy says we only need to do our usual routine. So you'll only be doing what you regularly do, only with more energy this time and of course with a million people watching. The audience has to be in a dancing frenzy when Ex-Man hits the stage. That's the way it is planned anyhow."

Frank was at a loss as to what to say next. "Do we get some complimentary tickets for friends?" he asked Trevor, his mind going to Sade.

"Sure. I'll ask the guys. It seems like the show is fully booked, but I'm sure they should be able to spare a few. How many do you want Frank?"

"I think two" Frank replied thinking one for Sade and maybe one of her friends.

"No worries Frank, they should be able to find you two tickets." Trevor was confident.

• • • • •

Ida called about an hour later, her voice low and hoarse like she was nursing a monster-size hangover; which she probably was.

"Have you got what I want on Harvey?" she asked.

"No Ida I don't yet have what you want on Harvey," Frank told her, wondering how she got his phone number. *Jeeezus!*

"How did you get my phone number?" he asked her. But Ida only groaned, this time in genuine pain.

"And why is that?" She asked, ignoring Frank's question.

"Because it's not as easy as you think. Harvey is one slippery fellow," he lied, "and it would be a lot easier if you kept those thugs that you sent, away from me," he added on a brainwave

"What thugs?" Ida sounded puzzled, to Frank's unhappiness.

"Well, some idiots chased me down my street and one of them I think, came back to rob my flat and very nearly knocked my head off with a vase."

"Poor you; they were not my thugs though, I assure you that," Ida told him.

"In any case, Harvey did come looking for me instead and promised to kill me if I couldn't find you. So could you please tell me where you are?" Frank pleaded.

"So you could have Harvey come in and kill me? Don't be ridiculous." Ida nervously replied.

"Well, if I can't find you, Harvey is going to kill me. So I guess I might as well tell you goodbye, the deal is off, I can't deliver. I'll locate you anyway because this conversation is recorded and I can trace your phone number," Frank lied to her. Ida abruptly ended the call.

•   •   •   •   •

Frank spent half of the next day at the crowded accident and emergency waiting room to have the attack to his head looked at. A doctor finally assured him that it was nothing serious and gave him some pills for his headache. The pills made him sleepy, and he did not wake up till night. Looking at a lonely night ahead, he decided to call Sade. He hadn't seen her since the exhibition at the Barbican the previous day. Sade's phone did not answer. It advised him instead to leave a message. Frank understood, she must be very tired.

He fired up his stereo, loaded it with an Ashford and Simpson CD and settled down to watch the football channel while eating a microwave frozen chow mein. Around eleven, he left a message on Sade's phone and went to sleep.

CHAPTER 18

Spencer left the conservatory and took a walk down the street. He felt like that bird in the cage; the bird that he had permitted to fly away. He bought a couple of hamburgers from a chip shop and ate as he took a stroll around. With Susan away in hospital, Spencer actually felt an extremely marvellous release, quite like the bird that flew away. And like the bird that flew away, Spencer resolved to pursue new vistas, previously forbidden places.

Spencer found himself in front of a seedy-looking pub called The Barking Dog. He had never before noticed this strange place. A dark and evil presence seemed to enshroud the neighbourhood. It was like being transported back to Victorian London when Jack the Ripper and Sweeney Todd roamed dangerously free. Spencer momentarily stopped to wonder, amused, who it was that suggested names to these pubs. Definitely a pack of retards, he decided.

A fist fight by drunken brawlers was in progress, and they were soon subdued and taken away by police. Spencer adventurously ventured inside. He ordered a beer and was almost immediately joined by a guy who had a vet jovial face and smile.

"Mind if I sit here with you mate?" the fellow asked

"No, not at all. Plenty of room here. My name is Spencer Cowley." He introduced himself, intending to make new friends.

"The name is Mark Currie; people here call me The Knife. Like Mark The Knife. What's an uptown guy like you doing in a place like this?" Mark Currie asked.

"I came for a drink, just like everybody else. I suppose," Spencer shrugged.

"Nah! Nah! Blokes like you come to this kind of place to get killed. Look all about you and tell me if you don't stand out like a rose in a box of mushroom" Mark laughed. Again Spencer shrugged.

"I don't have any problems with that." he replied.

"Look, I like this place, and I wouldn't wish to have any decent person die here, and get this place closed down, do you understand me?" Mark Currie sounded really worried.

"That is your problem sir; I can take care of myself," Spencer again said.

"Don't be so sure." Mark, at last, to decide to mind his business. Spencer bought Mark a beer.

"Why do they call you The Knife?" he was curious.

"Cause I done somebody with a knife, innit? Bloke was messing with my fiancé on my wedding eve. Didn't mean to kill him though, but you know how these things go especially after you've had a few beers." Mark drawled. Indeed, Spencer knew how these things went. He had nearly killed Susan, hadn't he?

•　　•　　•　　•　　•

Next day, Spencer called Victoria Collins, the producer of Murder Zone to suggest his Dennis Snow type of ending to one of the episodes

""It's got an amusing twist. Wicked old witch gets her just dessert after sixty years of tyranny, just because she served weak tea and her husband's fed up with having weak tea for sixty damned years and being too polite to say He's had enough," Victoria laughed,

""Yes. And Snow dies of a heart attack, just as the Ninja steps in. He thought it was the angel of death. Scared him to death ironically, without a single shot fired." Spencer added.

"Good; we'll use it.," he was happy to hear Victoria decide, and that made him more confident to ask a niggling question.

"Vickie, I've got a tough one here for another episode. It's quite a complicated plot. It's a love based thing, and I think women are better at love things," he said.

"Okay, shoot. Go ahead, I am listening" Victoria encouraged.

"It's got a lot of poetry too. You know, you can't have a love thing without poetry," Spencer continued

"Yuck! Okay, get it over with" Victoria Collins said.

The scenario is like this: This nice guy and this lovely lady fall in love and get married. But love soon suffers post nuptial demise. Are you still with me?

"Yep, ordinary story so far though; for most marriages love dies the next day as far as I know." Victoria yawned.

"Have a bit of patience, it gets better. Now ageing lovely lady falls in love again. But an ageing nice guy is not pleased. In fact, He's real pissed off about the whole situation, and He's thinking someone ought to get their just dessert. Now, if Romeo's going to get it, should he know why He's getting done? I mean should he know that it is because He's been messing with another man's wife? You know all that romantic stuff. I mean is that going to make the story more interesting?" Spencer said with genuine passion.

"I'll think about it. I'll kick it around me head a bit and call you in a few days" Victoria promised.

"Thanks dear. Love is cold. It distresses a straightforward crime," Spencer told her.

"Now, listen Spencer, don't do anything stupid, okay?" He thought Victoria sounded a bit worried.

"Nothing to worry about. You know me," Spencer assured her.

•　　•　　•　　•　　•

Next morning Spencer looked sadly around his cluttered office; he leaned back in his chair and closed his eyes. Somehow, he missed Frank, even though he was ashamed to admit it even to himself. Frank was like the irresponsible family bad boy, the one you constantly had to watch so that he didn't break something either intentionally or in error. Frank kept him watchful and on his toes every day, checking for faults to correct, because for some reasons Frank didn't seem able to do anything right while Spencer was watching. Now with Frank gone, he felt bored.

There were so few challenges left for him at the office. The sense of freedom he had acquired over the past few days, made this office feel like a dungeon into which he had attached himself by invisible chains. He now felt like he was slowly dying. He had worked for nearly eight years, trying to build a reputable newspaper. Now he wanted to be free. He wished he could just leave and never come back to this office.

On a shelf was his wedding photograph when he and Susan got married eight years back. She was a beautiful woman then, and she still was now. Susan loved to play; she used to be very lively. They went out a lot together and had great fun. Spencer wondered how and where their relationship had gone wrong.

Much of it he realised had to do with running a newspaper from scratch. His finances had consequently suffered a lot and left him working a lot more than he would have liked, just to be able to meet his bills, especially for keeping the newspaper alive. Irritability had been a secondary consequence and who else was there to bear most of the brunt other than poor Susan. The more the situations around him and his business frustrated him, the more irritable he became and the wider he and Susan drifted apart.

Spencer wished he could sell the newspaper. It was barely making a profit. Its only real asset was a lot of goodwill from satisfied readers and advertisers all over East London. How he wished he could sell the newspaper and spend more quality time with his wife. How he wished he and Susan could again be as happy as they had been in that photograph on the shelf.

● ● ● ● ●

Fernandez knocked and stuck his head through the doorway.

"You didn't forget our Monday morning meeting, did you? It is one hour late." Fernandez asked, jolting Spencer back to real life.

"No, I have not forgotten," he mumbled.

"You've never in the two years I have spent in this place forgotten Monday meetings" Fernandez pointlessly said.

"I will be with you in a few minutes" Spencer replied again shutting his eyes. At this moment and more than ever before he was also beginning to worry about the young man standing in the doorway of his office. Fernandez did almost everything perfectly like he could read your mind. He needn't be supervised like Frank. Even after he had fired Frank, Fernandez covered up so beautifully that it was difficult to see Frank was missing. But faultless workers eventually begin to get on your nerves, and Spencer had lately begun to fee that way about Fernandez.

"Is there anything wrong, Spencer?" Fernandez persisted. Spencer was startled to discover he was still standing there.

"I wish I could sell this fucking newspaper. I am tired, and I wish I could do something else. I wish I could find someone to buy me out?" Spencer said to himself

Taken completely by surprise, Fernandez backed out of Spencer's office.

•　　•　　•　　•　　•

Spencer found Mark Currie in the company of another man and a lady when he arrived at The Barking Dog that evening. Mark jovially introduced them as Roger the Rod, and Poison Ivy. All three seemed already drunk by the time Spencer arrived. Spencer sat with them and ordered more beer all around. One more round later he thought he finally had the friendly attention of his new friends.

"What would you do to a person, intending to mess with your wife?" he asked

"I'll give him the knife. He'll die slowly and painfully" Mark Currie was sure. He spoke from experience.

"No, no. When you stick people with a knife, they yell like crazy. It's only on television that people die silently when you stick them. It's only on television and stupid love films." Spencer disagreed.

"That's right. Only in stupid love films." Ivy Arrowood alias Poison Ivy agreed

"Big deal. He won't be making much noise if you slit his throat" Mark persisted, indeed very drunk

"You drunk sod. All that blood gushing out onto your hand, you must be crazy. What you need is a gun. Just shoot him. Bang; the end." Roger intervened.

"Yes, the gun option looks attractive but it lacks elegance. Nevertheless, it looks like a dramatic way to conclude a story. Just shoot the fucker. Bang! The end." Spencer's laugh roared even louder than with the rest.

"I have got a pistol with a silencer. It's a real gun. Bloke pawned it and got himself killed up in Hackney, so I am stuck with the gun I can give it to you for fifty quid" Roger confided in them all.

"Guns are so common. Poison does a better job if you ask me. I've done three boyfriends so far, and they'll never forget me for the rest of their lives. You know why? Cause they are dead, that's why." Ivy was not impressed.

"You're wasting your time. I'd cut out his heart like a dog." Mark Currie insisted.

It was a fantastic night for Spencer. He'd certainly had a lot more fun discussing with Mark, Roger, and Ivy, than he ever had doing same with Fred Duffy. A good murder was an art; the motive, the means, and the method must seamlessly fit together. At this night's discussion, what they were doing was attempting to settle the matter of the motive, the means, and the method. Only that Fred Duffy would never know about it.

•   •   •   •   •

Fred Duffy came visiting next evening, looking very sad. Spencer got him a beer as usual

"How have you been Fred? I'd say though that you don't look too good" Spencer asked

"Thank you, Spencer, I've had quite a bad week" Fred replied.

"Yes, so have we all. Stupid rain keeps falling, and what with Susan still stuck in hospital. "Spencer agreed. A jubilant thought danced in his mind though. : You will soon starve to death Fred won't you? I mean there isn't going to be any more cobblers and trifle for you for a long time. Just think about that, and doesn't it make you feel desperate Fred? Death by starvation is one means that we have not yet looked at. Imagine that Fred. Death by starvation. That was what the they said.

"Poor Susan." Fred sorrowfully drank his beer.

"Never mind, she will soon be out. Let's get down to more urgent business Fred. Look there's this scenario that's just cropped up. It is a situation with a heavy love theme, but I am not very good at the love thing in stories. I am sure you're a lot better than me with all that jazz. Do you, for example, think it is okay to administer euthanasia to a half-willing person. You know, out of love?" Spencer asked. Fred slowly shook her head and sighed, tiredly.

"That is pure murder. Nobody can ever get away with it. Listen Spencer, I don't want to play these games anymore. It's not doing you any good either. I went to see Susan at the hospital yesterday. She Hasn't seen you all week, and she's very worried about you."

"I've been busy," Spencer airily replied, to Fred's astonishment.

"You can't be too busy to visit your wife in hospital, Spencer. Susan also says that I should try and get you to see Dr. Maxwell. The doctor says he Hasn't seen you for months. You've been missing your appointments.""

"I don't want to see any fuckin' psychiatrist. There's nothing the matter with me" Spencer exploded, striding dangerously around inside the conservatory

"Dr. Maxwell doesn't seem to agree. You see, He's also worried about you," Fred Duffy insisted. Spencer stopped, obviously startled.

"You've been sneaking behind me to go talk to my doctor? I can't believe this. I bet you also think already that I should be locked away in a mental hospital; right?" he growled.

"Nothing of that sort Spencer. It just happens that Dr. Maxwell lives two houses away from me and somehow knows that I visit your house. I don't know how he knew that." Fred defensively replied.

"How convenient. Okay. I will see Susan in the morning. Are you satisfied?" he snarled at Fred.

•　　•　　•　　•　　•

Spencer saw Fred out the door and dashed into his study. Suddenly the plot against him became very clear. He could now see the entire secret plan unfolding. Susan had a lot of foresight about this guy, Spencer concurred. Fred Duffy was certainly going to cause him trouble. He was angry at how he had been so unfairly rewarded. He brought this person into his home, gave him his dinners and his beer; but He's not satisfied with that; he wanted his wife too, and he wanted her so badly, he would have him put away in a mental hospital to get her.

Spencer opened a desk drawer. He brought out a pistol and admired it; Roger Fanshaw alias The Rod had given it to him this afternoon. Spencer wondered how big a hole it would blast in Fred Duffy's head.

The sudden ring of his phone alarmed him so much that the gun dropped on the floor. Spencer hurriedly picked it up and tucked it deep into the back of the drawer before picking up the phone.

"Is this Spencer Cowley?" an unfamiliar voice asked.

"Yes it is Spencer Cowley; who are you?" he also asked, his voice shaky.

"My name is Moses Samuel and I have a proposition I believe is going to make you very happy," the voice told him.

CHAPTER 19

Nancy Hughes was sitting in a coffee shop in Woodgreen one evening, looking so lost and completely deflated when Sasha Cohen found her. They became very close friends within a few more days, even as Sasha introduced her to the tranquility of Woodstock. Here Sasha took her on a voyage of discovery both of the spiritual kind and all around the London art scene. And before Nancy knew it, they had become lovers, and Nancy did not care anymore.

Nancy's desperate call to Frank had been the result of a panic that had one morning surfaced to torment her - the frightful thought that she might not be able to fall in love with a man anymore. Being with Sasha wasn't really so bad anyway.

They had been walking in the City this afternoon, she and Sasha, when they'd come across an ethnic fashion exhibition going on at the Barbican. It was quite an unusual display that they had been easily drawn into it. Several minutes later, Nancy had found himself at a particular stand, primarily because she'd seen Frank leaving that place. And she had been interested in the African lady who had affectionately kissed him before he left. She needed to know who this lady was.

Sade had been very much curious of the two kooky white ladies who had come visiting her exhibition – one wearing a black dress, lots of beads around her neck and genuine John Lennon sunglasses. The other was more sanely dressed in jeans and a flower print top. Nevertheless, she was also generously beaded up around the neck.

They'd talked very excitedly about her display for several minutes, and at Nancy's suggestion, Sasha had invited Sade for dinner at a restaurant on Cheapside, not too far away. Sade had joined them after the close of the event in the evening and on the basis of their promise to put some business her way. The evening had thereafter coasted along very nicely on the wheels of two bottles of fine wine.

"We are building up a new and unusual shopping mart, and I think you could be part of this; you've got the sort of stuff we need. You've also got the sort of talent that we need. Yes, I think your display could find a home with us. The Rabbi would be thrilled to meet with you," Sasha told her.

Sade was quite piqued by the "Rabbi" bit. She was also curious to learn more about his unusual shopping mart, only Sasha wasn't saying.

"I can only say so much; the Rabbi makes the final decisions" Sasha explained to her.

•   •   •   •   •

Sasha suggested for Sade to meet her boss Moses Samuel at Woodstock that very night. And Sade had said yes, why not. Both of her two new friends looked kooky, but she didn't feel any danger being with them. In fact, Sasha was quite fun to be with.

When Sade met Moses Samuel, she was as surprised as Ex-Man had been under similar circumstances. The wine had made all of them a bit giggly, and she wished they had brought some along with them, but as she learned alcohol was not permitted in Woodstock. Inside Moses Samuel's office and sipping a mug of herbal tea, she sat later that night to endure a more thorough description of the offer, which was done with the aid of a slide show. Sade loved it all. It was so exciting, and she thought she would have paid to be part of this.

"How do I get home?" she'd asked Sasha after the discussion.

"You needn't go home tonight. There will be a lot to do from tomorrow morning and the earlier we get started, the better. Best for you to stay here; we've got lots of room here, and you can go home to pack a bag tomorrow. You will be staying here for some time, at least till after the opening," Sasha told her.

"Not a problem," Sade said with a big yawn. She was tired and all she needed tonight was a long sleep.

•   •   •   •   •

The next day was certainly busy. They had long meetings with architects, interior decorators, and a dozen or so other parties, and even though Sade still didn't know where the shopping mart would be, she knew nevertheless that it would be an exciting place to visit. It was night before she realized that she still hadn't called Frank. She looked for her phone but couldn't find it. She remembered that before she left the Barbican, she had asked Lolade, her cousin and sort of assistant, to take all the exhibition stuff to her place. She now remembered that she had left her phone inside the swatch bag.

"I've really got to get in contact with Frank. He is going to be worried "; Sade very honestly told Sasha and Nancy.

"Frank? Anyone, we know?" Nancy asked with a wry smile.

"Oh no, you wouldn't know Frank O'Dwyer," Sade said with a yawn. Another tiring day. "Can I borrow your phone?"

"Sure," said Sasha, going off to get her phone.

"You love him so much, don't you?" Nancy could no more restrain herself. Sade hummed yes.

"But does he love you that much? Men have quite massive ego problems you know," Sasha returning, offered.

"Not my Frank" Sade assured them.

"How would you like to find out how much he loves you then?"

"I don't need to find out, I already know."

"So you wouldn't mind to find out then, just to make sure that what you already know is true?"

"Certainly not, but it would just be a waste of time. I know my Frank. Look, let's stop talking about this. Can I use your phone?"

"Okay, let's do it this way," Sasha said after what seemed like a long thought. And she told her the zaniest plan she'd ever heard in her life.

"I know Frank O'Dwyer," Nancy finally threw in her confession.

"You do? What a coincidence," Sade was truly surprised.

"Yes I did, we used to live together."

"Oh, you are the Nancy that left him a note then? What a coincidence" Sade couldn't hide her surprise.

"Me and you would have a lot to talk about for the next few days then since we have something, or should I say someone in common," Nancy laughed.

"You did know her boyfriend?" Sasha sounded hurt.

"Yes, I did Sasha; a long time ago. Not sure if I know him anymore though. We've both fallen in love with someone else," Nancy said; taking Sasha's hand in hers.

Sade gave the phone back to Sasha. She decided it was the most important thing in the world to get to the bottom of this business going on between Nancy and Frank.

CHAPTER 20

In the Boar's Head pub at Mile End, three men were holding a night council. They were Bill Mulligan, Andy Wagstaff, and Michael Barlow; all of them from Harvey Simpson's work gang. Harvey had been progressively deteriorating, which was a real problem to the three men since much of their regular work and therefore income came through Harvey. Together, they envisaged the unpleasant situation when Harvey would go into another drinking binge, as had happened a couple of times earlier and subsequently end up again in rehab. And when that occurred, where would they go for work except the Jobcenter.

Over the years, Harvey had become to them their brain, eyes, and hands because Harvey knew about paperwork. Harvey could negotiate contracts, and he could understand agreements, and he had an office kitted out with people who could type out stuff and could work with figures. Harvey had an organization which made sure business progressed, even when Harvey went funny in the head for a couple of days. But all this, they knew, didn't take away the stark truth which was Harvey was the brain of Groundhog Groundwork Contracting Limited. Quite a shame that Harvey had permitted a pesky woman to get into his head and mess it up.

"You think the woman finally done a bunk on him at last?"

"Fuck me, how do I know? But we've got a real problem on our hands is all that matters. Harvey is going to end up again in a bender and me, and you all are going to be up the creek, as usual, is all I know" Bill Mulligan threw up his hands.

"So, what do you suggest we do? I mean telling Harvey to lay off the booze isn't going to work. So I see two alternatives. Either we find his wife, or we find another employer very quickly," Andy Wagstaff grimly suggested.

"Sounds so easy, innit? Harvey has been our mainstay for more than five years now and have you tried to find work in winter? It's terribly difficult as you know, but Harvey always gets us fixed all the time. So now He's got a bit of problem, you want us to dump him. You are a silly twat, that's what you are." Michael clearly did not agree.

"Well, it was just a suggestion. I guess the other alternative is for us to find Ida for him then."

"I knew that woman would be trouble as soon as I set my eyes on her. He met her at Alcoholics Anonymous too. I mean what sort of woman goes to AA? Only Harvey had to be mad enough to marry her," Bill Mulligan was thoroughly miserable.

"We've got to find Ida. Any suggestion on where to start, Bill?" Michael asked.

"Fuck me, how do I know? For all you know, she's shacked up with some bloke somewhere, getting shagged and getting piss drunk all day long," Bill said.

"Maybe she's dead," Harvey said.

"Not likely. If she's dead, the next-of-kin would have been notified. And the next-of-kin, in this case, is Harvey, innit?" Michael was certain.

"Well, she could be lying dead in the woods somewhere, strangled to death by a rapist and murderer. It happens sometimes you know" Andy persisted.

"Shut up you silly dickhead. She isn't dead, she's missing," Michael rebuked.

"Well she could be dead and missing," Andy held his ground. Michael resolved to ignore him.

"Bill, we've got to do something about this. I mean we have to find Ida. I had a chat with Harvey couple of days ago, and he said he'd hired a detective to find her. Harvey was plastered as usual of course, so I don't know for certain if this is true. Do you have any idea who this detective could be Bill; I mean assuming he exists."

"Fuck me"; Bill Mulligan shrugged his massive shoulders.

"Why do you say fuck me all the time you big ox; you gone gay or something?" Andy yelled at him.

"Fuck me; yeah I am gay or something; that is why I got myself married twice and got myself taken to the cleaners twice. Yeah, gay of course; that's me, you idiot. I need to chop off my dick, that's what," Bill morosely told the.

"In any case, we need to help Harvey out. I will get him to tell me who the detective is and we will persuade the bloke to work for us," Michael suggested.

"You mean we should force him to work for us? Better if we did this with money though. You can't always go around, bashing people's heads in and expect them to work for you. How much do you think we should offer this detective bloke? Ten quid?"

"Ten quid?! I wouldn't go find a cat lost its way home for ten quid. That's the kind of money you give to a drunk in a pub" Andy was incredulous.

"So what do you think is adequate then?" Michael was still ignoring Andy.

"Fuck me, how do I know," Bill shrugged.

"Yeah fuck you, what do you know," Andy affirmed.

"I don't care what you think. I am not forking out ten quid to find any woman," Bill remained obstinate.

●　　●　　●　　●　　●

In her entire life, Sade had never been as close to as many stars in one place as she saw at Woodstock. It seemed like whichever direction she turned there was a celebrity to be seen. At breakfast in the restaurant the next morning, she could count at least ten in the large, sparsely populated room and those were the ones that she could recognize. She was sure the rest were equally and probably more important. There were music stars, football stars, film stars, politicians, businesspersons and the ubiquitous professional celebrities who did nothing else for a living. Some were huddled together conversing in hushed tones, and some sitting alone lost in their own minds.

Breakfast was nothing to get excited about. The buffet table was filled with vegetable salads, fruit salads, mixed nuts, fruits and fruit juices, vegetables and vegetable juices, brown bread and herbal teas. It seemed a spread to torture a normal palate with, and a lot more people in the restaurant appeared to also have that impression, considering the gloomy look on their faces. Nevertheless, they had paid huge amounts to be here and seemed determined to get detoxified of the rich foods with which they had poisoned their bodies. They were all handling the ordeal quite magnificently. Sade helped herself to some fruit salad, a handful of mixed nuts and mug of rosebush tea with honey. She still had no idea where Sasha and Nancy were and was in no mood to go looking for them. Instead, she decided to do some exploration on her own.

Woodstock was a huge place as she found; the grounds stretching as far as her eyes could see. She would learn later that much of it was still farmland which supplied organically grown food for the health spa. The lawns and hedges had been carefully manicured. There were small fields of fragrant flowers, and there were smooth-pebbled walks which were a bit uncomfortable for Sade to walk on since like everyone else she had met so far, she also didn't have her shoes on. There were huge buildings that housed courts for tennis, squash, and badminton and a vast gymnasium. All of the many staff at Woodstock dressed in white loosely cut soft cotton tunics which flapped even in the lazy breeze.

Her exploration took her to an open hall where a lecture was in progress. The audience was sitting on mats on the floor in front of the speaker whom she recognized as Moses Samuel. The lecture was about humane treatment of all animals and all living things. Sade found a mat and got seated, crossing her legs like most of the others. The handsome little lady next to her, and also the man who appeared to be her companion appeared to be having more than a bit of trouble with this sitting position, preferring to sit hugging their knees to the chest. They were clearly new here.

"Hi, I am Ida," the small lady whispered to her, with a grimace. It definitely was an uncomfortable sitting position.

"My name is Sade," she replied. Ida looked at her curiously, apparently trying to decide if she looked anything like the music star she knew. Ida eventually gave her a thumb up and switched her attention to the lecture.

•　　•　　•　　•　　•

"When we kill other living beings for no reason, it brutalizes them as much as it brutalizes us as human beings. Consequently, they learn to kill other living beings for no reason, and eventually, the vicious cycle returns to us in the form of more vicious human societies, more vicious pests and predators, and more vicious diseases. If we are able to break this terrible cycle somewhere, there could just yet be hope for humanity in the future. But will this happen? Not likely; I tell you big business - the most vicious predator out there, will not permit it. But we must never lose hope; we must continue to strive to cut the excesses of big business, which unfortunately employs many of you either directly or indirectly. We must reject the poisonous products being irresponsibly peddled by big business, and we must by this means starve that monster to death."

Moses Samuel was really a gifted and sincere speaker, and the lecture could have well been a religious event. So rapt was the attention of the listeners. The lecture was finally concluded, with a loud ovation. A long-haired male staff who seemed to have higher spiritual responsibility in this place, stood in front of the audience to tell them that the Rabbi Zulu, the spiritual leader at Woodstock would be available for consultation later in the day by appointment.

●   ●   ●   ●   ●

The soft, soul-stirring sound of sitars soon filled the room as a yoga instructor replaced Moses Samuel who had now left the room together with a small retinue of staff. Sade decided again to endure the yoga session. The breathing exercise actually did her a lot of good, and she left the hall thirty minutes later slightly light-headed and feeling a lot healthier.

The small lady and her friend caught up with her,

"Hi, I am Ida. Are you someone famous too?" she eagerly enquired.

"Not yet, but I am working on it," Sade liked her immediately. She had that pure, sinless aura all around her.

"Me too," Ida giggled. Her friend offered Sade a handshake.

"Hi, I am Jimmy; he said.

"Nice to meet you Jimmy; nice to meet you Ida," Sade cheerfully responded.

"Are you a guest? I mean are you a paying guest? You must be pretty loaded "; Ida prodded, and quite convinced that you needed to be somebody to be here in Woodstock.

"Not a paying guest I must again disappoint you; I was invited here by a friend who works here."

"Same as me. My friend Phil...Oops, I mean the owner Rabbi Zulu, said I could stay here as long as I wanted. I am hiding away from someone who wants to kill me, you know," Ida confided.

"Ida," Jimmy admonished, at which Ida clapped her hand over her mouth and hasted away after Jimmy, turning around to give Sade a thumb up as she went.

Sade eventually found Nancy and Sasha as they came out of the restaurant.

"There you are; come we've got a lot to do today," Sasha said leading her away by the hand.

"Have you ever met the Ex-Man?" Sasha asked Sade.

"No; is he here too?" Sade asked.

"In a couple of hours. You are in for a treat," Sasha laughed.

CHAPTER 21

Raj again called Frank two days later.

"I've got the money for you," Raj announced.

"What money?" Frank asked him, pretending not to understand.

"Two hundred thousand pounds in a briefcase. The bad people, the kidnappers of my daughter, they want you to bring the money to Liverpool Street station at noon tomorrow. After that they let my daughter go."

"They want me to? Why me?" Frank again asked him.

"Because it is your job," Raj replied.

"I wouldn't wish to put my life in unnecessary jeopardy. I only signed up to find your stolen lucky charm. To do dangerous stuff like delivering ransom money will cost you fifty thousand," Frank told Raj, figuring if he could find two hundred, he certainly could find fifty thousand more."

"You damn crook; go to hell. Before you said fifteen thousand," Raj raved at the other end.

"The price of insurance just went up. But no problem, you needn't pay me all that money. You can deliver it yourself then," Frank told him.

"No, I will not deliver the money, you silly man. It is your job to deliver money" Raj railed.

"No can do," Frank told him and ended the call.

Raj was the least of his worries today. For three days and since the exhibition ended Frank hadn't heard from Sade. Six times he'd called and left messages on the phone yet no sign of her. No message, no calls, and her flat was locked with a stack of junk mail at the door, assuring that she hadn't visited recently. Frank called a couple of her friend with no luck. Her cousin Lolade informed that Sade had met up with some customers for dinner three days ago and also hadn't heard from her since. Frank thought of calling the police but then wondered how he would sound – quite like Raj insisting his daughter had been kidnapped when she could be holed up with a lover somewhere. That thought was like a sharp dagger through Frank's heart: *a lover somewhere.*

When Frank's phone rang again, he was in a murderous mood and could have strangled Raj this time had he been within reach.

"I tell you I am not going to deliver any fucking money, do you understand?" he shouted into the phone. But it wasn't Raj.

"Frank?" Sade's voice came to him instead. And she sounded tired and desperate.

"Frank?" she said again, and the phone was abruptly cut off.

CHAPTER 22

Moses Samuel came to see him at the office next morning in the company of a plump lady who wore a bright, flowered frock and John Lennon sunglasses. Both had outlandish appearances, but Spencer Cowley always could recognise serious money whenever it came near him.

David Fernandez came in together with the visitors, and Spencer waved him away.

"No, let him stay; my visit concerns him," Moses Samuel insisted. Spencer shrugged.

"So what can I do for you, Mr. Samuel? You mentioned a business proposal" Spencer asked after the three were seated.

"I will be very brief, and I hopefully wish this wouldn't be a wasted journey. Mr. Cowley, I want to buy your newspaper," Spencer told him. Spencer was for a long minute silent; taking time to digest the offer and also determine if the outlandish person before him was serious.

"And what gave you the impression I want to sell?" Spencer feebly hedged.

"I told him you mentioned to me you wished you could sell the newspaper," Fernandez came in.

"I was just speaking aloud to myself, wasn't I?" Spencer mumbled

"So, you don't really want to sell then," Moses Samuel seemed about to get up

"Yes I certainly could be persuaded to sell, depending on what you are offering," Spencer quickly said.

"How much do you want for your newspaper, Mr. Cowley?"

"I'd rather have you make me an offer. I wouldn't want to scare you away." Spencer maneuvered.

From behind the dark aviator sunglasses, Moses Samuel's eyes seemed in an attempt to read Spencer's mind

"I will give you a million and a half," Moses Samuel told Spencer. He didn't wait for a reply; he slipped a card across Spencer's table.

"Call me if you like my offer," he said. He shook hands with Spencer and left with his partner.

"Is he serious? "Spencer would ask Fernandez after they were gone.

"I am sure he is serious. He can afford it," Fernandez confirmed.

●　　●　　●　　●　　●

Two mornings later, Spencer Cowley began to pack all his personal together from his office at East End Mirror. He hummed happily as he went about the difficult task of selecting what to take along with him and what should go in the bin. Eight years of his life had been spent in this office and nearly everything, even the notepads he considered valuable. In the end, he resolved to only remove no more than would fit into a small box and then he would instruct Ellen Wescott to shred the rest. Eventually, all he decided to rescue was Susan's photograph; the one he had taken with her at their wedding.

At the door, Spencer Cowley gave a final salute in an imitation of Frank O'Dwyer. But nobody was there to return his salute. It was Sunday, and the office was not open for work. That was how he wanted to leave; with no hugs, no tears and no fanfare. He would break the news to them all the next morning with a phone call.

With a million and a half pounds in the bank, the television reality show Spencer Cowley was developing became unimportant. He certainly didn't need the money from that; not anymore. He called Fred Duffy and without telling him why took him on a celebratory visit to The Barking Dog. There they all had a wild night together with Roger, Mark, and Ivy. Somewhere along that night Ivy found Fred very interesting to talk with and so did Fred also think about her.

Three nights down the line and Spencer was satisfied to see a love affair between Fred Duffy and Ivy blossom before his eyes. He was satisfied that all things being equal whatever flash affection that could have been between Fred and Susan would now be in the past. He also hoped that Ivy Arrowood would eventually poison Fred Duffy as she had her previous boyfriends.

Susan would be out of hospital in about a week. She had been ecstatic to learn that the newspaper had been sold for so much. She was also pleased to agree with Spencer that they should sell the house and buy a quiet place in Winchester where Susan had always dreamed to live, and then go on a pleasure trip round the world.

CHAPTER 23

Sam "The Snake" Donahue was feeling a lot better when Frank saw him at the hospital next days. He still seemed quite in a bit of pain from the way he talked, but his arms and legs were no longer up in the scaffold

"Hey you are back," he hoarsely said; his crooked smile looked more like a grimace.

"Yes, how are you? Seemed like a truck ran you over that last time I came here to see you along with Maureen?" Frank told him.

"I feel great I think. My head still hurts like a motherfucker though," he said.

"Did you get a good look at the blokes who messed you up? The police ought to be able to get them brought in. I mean they could have killed you," Frank asked him.

Sam shook his head. "I did get a good look at them, but I am not telling. In fact, I got a good look at them for a whole hour. Mind you, I don't really know them, at least not socially. They came to my auction and decided they sort of didn't like my system. Those bastards nearly killed me."

"Oh well, they did lose a lot of money to you didn't they? I know how these auctions go, and I've lost a hundred once. Maybe these guys found it less funny than I did," Frank told him.

"Not that I took the money out of their pockets myself did I?" Sam remained self-righteous.

"Anyway, it seems like you won't be doing any selling for a while the way I see it. Looks like you going to be here for a couple of weeks at least."

"Never mind I need the rest anyway. It is not costing me anything to stay here. In fact, when I get out, I'll retire from the auction business. I think I will start an estate agency instead. Less risk of being beaten up in that. Or I start a money lending business, and I do the beating up. Now, what brings you here, aye?" Sam asked.

"Well, I've still got that case sitting right on top of my mind all the time and getting more complicated every day the way I see it. I was wondering what did you think the Barefoot Revolution, or whatever you said it was called, could have had to do with all this."

"Oh, you mean the Barefoot Revolution? I thought I already got back to you on that. Listen, I have a friend who lives up in Brixton. Polish bloke called Casper whatever." Sam gave him Casper's phone number. Frank patted him on the leg cast and left the ward.

"I wish I could go out and smoke a cigarette though" He could hear Sam grumble as he left.

•   •   •   •   •

Frank called Casper, and he suggested meeting me the next day at the Brixton Oval. Again, Frank had not yet heard a word from Sade since the last brief call. Constantly though, he battled with the option of becoming the wimpy boyfriend who went to make a missing girlfriend report to the police.

Frank went to Brixton next day. Casper suggested they meet at noon, but since he had a lot of time to kill in the morning, he went to do a bit of sun-worship at Clapham Park, where he sat eating potato chips and ice cream he'd bought from a nearby shop. His eyes were briefly arrested by the two lovers strolling by. He had his arm lovingly around her; she had her hand in his back pocket. Bitch; Frank thought. An effeminate lad subtly attempted to show Frank his own naked pictures from the screen of a mobile phone. Shocked back to reality, Frank looked at his wristwatch and found it was still about an hour to his appointment. Nevertheless, he felt the need to leave immediately.

Clapham Commons was not familiar territory, and not willing to risk an unwanted trip in the wrong direction, he sought the opinion of the nearest bystander at the bus stop - a black lady dressed up in a white trouser suit and a white tasseled fez with gold trimmings. She looked like a fortune teller or a magician's apprentice and appeared quite impatient to get her large suitcase into a bus and to the next gig.

"Can you tell me what bus goes to Brixton?" Frank asked Madame Zizzi.

"You need 37," she impatiently replied. Feeling an urgent need to distrust this advice, Frank consulted the route map on a board inside the bus shelter.

"No" I don't think so. Bus 37 goes to Peckham. I'm sure 35, 45 or 345 will do a better job"", Frank disagreed with Madame Zizzi

She looked affronted.

"So why did you ask me then, if you knew which bus to take?" she rebuked, screwing a stiff finger to her head.

"Well I thought you might know," Frank apologized.

"Of course, I know; you are the one who's lost innit?" Madame Zizzi gloated.

"Thanks all the same," Frank told her.

Thankfully the 45 bus arrived at this moment and took Madame Zizzi away to her infernal destination. Bus 35 was also not too far behind. It was crowded, but since Brixton was merely ten minutes away Frank reasoned there was no need to wait for another bus, so he hopped on.

●　　●　　●　　●　　●

Ras Taba was sitting on the aisle side of the only available seat on the lower deck of the bus. Ras Taba may not have been his real name of course, but it was the name that occurred to Frank. He certainly looked like an eponymous friend of Trevor from a long way back in high school, though now in a more dangerous way. Ras Taba was staring blankly through the window at some unseen wonders; he appeared completely oblivious of whatever went on around him. There was an empty seat beside Ras Taba and being able to find an empty seat in the packed bus quite thrilled Frank.

"Can you move so that I can have this seat," Frank asked him.

Ras Taba brought suddenly back to life looked first, as if in trance, at Frank's face and then contemplated the one-foot distance by which he would need to move his ass to permit someone else to sit beside him. The required effort appeared quite daunting.

"Go upstairs," he dozily indicated with his head. "Why you telling a black man to move like eighteenth-century colonial slave master? Go upstairs," he suggested.

"No I'd rather not go upstairs. Don't worry I'll stand; my stop is not quite far away." Frank very cheerfully told him. But Ras Taba was unrepentant. He shrugged and went back to gazing through the window.

Ras Taba changed his mind, a couple of minutes later, and invited Frank to take the inner seat, but Frank declined. He didn't trust this guy at all. For a long minute thereafter, Ras Taba kept looking Frank over, then he touched Frank's BHS Khaki jacket, fingering the fabric.

"I never seen a coat like this since second world war. What patrol did they put you in, blood?" he taunted. "

"Lion killers," Frank nervously replied

"*Lah-yan Killahs.*" Ras Taba amusedly echoed; dutifully resuming his romance with the window. The bus soon arrived at Brixton stop, and Frank disembarked. Ras Taba also came down alongside.

"Oi mate, can you tell me where the Brixton Library is?" Frank asked him.

"I look like gay to you?" Ras Taba rebuked taking a wary step backward.

"Of course not. I am trying to locate Brixton Oval; I learn it is in front of the library" Frank laughed uneasily."

"Oh; the place where they keep them book ting," comprehension appeared finally to Ras Taba, and he indicated with his head. "It's over there man. "

Over there, was a concrete paved court about a fifth of the size of a football field, right in front of an ancient edifice that was the Brixton Library. A man in a string vest and hideous sunglasses was doing complicated pirouettes on roller skates. A miscreant was playing loud tinny music from a mobile phone and simultaneously having a loud and angry argument with another phone. Pockets of idlers aimlessly milled around, engaged in one form of non-activity or the other. A couple of police patrols stood menacingly in sight, but some recalcitrant stragglers nevertheless defiantly shared fat ganja cigarettes; the fragrant smoke wafting lazily over the open place.

Frank considered going into the library; it certainly looked a lot cooler inside, and he still had about half an hour to kill before his appointment with Casper. His indecision was put to rest by a rowdy exchange of greetings nearby. A uniformed African street cleaner dutifully trundling his dustcart along, was being hailed by a West Indian and Polish pair sitting on a bench.

"Erasmus, come down here, will you; lots of rubbish here," the Pole was yelling.

"*Dzien dobry* .What you doing there Casper? Get off your ass and look busy or else You'll get the sack," Erasmus morosely replied.

"Fuck off, it's my day off," the Pole laughed.

"Street cleansers shouldn't get days off, *rass*. You idiots want London to smell? Take five minutes off Erasmus; you look like you dead already," the West Indian advised.

"Yes, do as Fish says and take a break, Erasmus. You leave your house too early in the morning before anyone wakes up and you are not back by the time anyone goes to sleep. Come sit with us for a while; then maybe I take you to the cinema and then the pub later. You only have one life you know," Casper said.

"Cinema? You expect me to sit with you in a cinema and then in a pub and just waste my life doing nothing?" Erasmus sounded incredulous.

"Leave the man alone Casper; the man come to this world to sweep London; That's the purpose of his life. Isn't that right Erasmus?" Fish said wickedly.

Erasmus stuck a finger rudely in his face.

"I do not understand why anyone comes to this country; it is cold unfriendly and so expensive," he sulked.

"So why you come here then; to see the Queen?" Fish asked.

Fish looked quite like Pork Pie from the old time television series *Desmond's* and Frank could almost hear the *soca* music just by looking at him.

"Yeah Erasmus," Casper said. "You should have stayed home. Things can't be much better there for all I know; else all of you wouldn't be coming here by the planeload everyday."

"My country is exactly the opposite, Fish. It is warm, friendly and cheap; and certainly a lot more civilized."

"Civilized? You need to be civilized to become a street sweeper in London; you went crazy man," Fish laughed.

"Crazy is what I said I've become; they don't even like me here. I am a nuisance."

"Yeah man, fuck off; go back home to your country. I don't like you either," Fish told him.

"I only wish people would learn to be kind to immigrants; after all, nobody had a choice of where they wanted to be born or whom their parents should be. They should learn to try and understand why they come here," Erasmus philosophized.

"This is the place you come to make progress with your life isn't it?" Fish reminded.

"I doubt it Fish. Look at you; almost all your life you spent here, and you can't even speak proper English. You call that making progress with your life?" Erasmus didn't agree.

"Yeah man; let me be. At least I speak better English than stupid Casper here from bloody Warsaw; *bloodclat*"

"Yeah man; *bloodclat*," Casper mimicked.

"I was an accountant you know," Erasmus boasted. "I swear by the head of Charlie's mother I studied Accountancy in university"

"You swear by the head of Charlie's mother?" Casper appeared confused,

"Bloodclat is talking about money. You know the system got the head of the Queen on the money, and the Queen is Prince Charlie's mother. Seen?" Fish explained. "

"So what happened to your own mother then? Very convenient to swear by the head of somebody else's mother" Casper scolded.

"As a matter of fact, my mother would die of a heart attack if she learned of what I do here. I told her I worked for the council, but certainly not as a street cleaner. I must have been crazy to come to this bloody country. Back home I had respect" Erasmus agonized.

"Respect doesn't put money in your pocket, friend," Casper pointed out.

"Yeah man; every day he complains, but he never goes back home," Fish said.

"Okay, I don't have a job to return home to," Erasmus conceded. "And I have a family to take care of. But I swear if any of them ever saw me on this job they will die of the shame."

"You know sometimes I think this television and cinema ting is to trick black people to come to England. See how they come across to you, man. London, the most beautiful place in the world; London, the richest city in the world. Come to London, and you will return home with enough money to spend for the rest of your life. You will ride the biggest cars, live in the biggest houses; get all the beautiful girls," Fish ruefully shook his head.

"I would have said that sounds like a good enough reason to do anything," Casper laughed.

"Yeah man," Fish agreed. "Unfortunately, it's sixteen years since I got here. Sixteen years and all I have seen so far is filth and harassment. Everywhere there is Babylon," he said morosely.

"Babylon? Why do you always call them Babylon? The police is your friend Fish; they like you," Erasmus chuckled.

It was Fish's turn to give him a stiff finger.

"You know it's like slavery days again, man? Only this time they hand out candy; they give you eye candy to make you come here by yourself; instead of bringing you in chains. It's the new slavery," Fish agonized.

"That's not quite right you know. Look at me I've been here only four years, and it is not so bad really," Casper told them.

"And so you will be a star when you eventually return home then. You'll speak the best English in Warsaw. Probably get you medals then," Erasmus was sarcastic.

"I'm not going back to Warsaw; I like living here. It's nice," Casper confided.

"Nice; you call this nice? This place is evil. Nobody talks to anyone else. You could go fucking mad here you know" Fish snorted.

"Worse in Warsaw. It is much colder, and you could get killed for laughing at all. In fact, people get killed every day for being happy at all" Casper disagreed. "

"Wow, I never thought there was a more terrible place than this. This is the worst country in the world, man," Erasmus said wondrously.

"So when are you going back home, *rass*?" Fish asked.

"Before next winter I swear. One more winter here and I am ready for the place where they put mad people" Erasmus told him.

"Every year you say that," Fish sneered.

"I swear by the head of Charlie's mother," Erasmus took a pound coin from his pocket and bit on it in an oath.

"What's wrong with your own mother then? Why can't you swear by the head of your own mother?" Fish taunted.

"Do you see my mother's head on any currency?" Erasmus scowled.

"Meaning what?" Casper sneered.

"Meaning I am only here for the money. You think I came to see bloody Buckingham Palace like you nincompoops? "

"Yeah man, I miss Jamaica. You know what I've been eating for many days now man? Greasy fried chicken and potato chips. Now does that look like black man's food to you? Nice to have a decent meal every day without spending an arm and a leg," Fish shook his head ruefully. "

"Back home people call me by my name. Here, I am just a forgettable face; no one knows my real name." Erasmus persisted in his grief.

"Your name is Erasmus; or have you forgotten?" Fish pointed out.

"No sir, I call myself Erasmus because nobody can pronounce my real name. Here I am just another nameless hungry immigrant. I'm sure Casper is not your real name either."

Casper was non-committal.

"So go back home then. Stop whining and go home" he said to Erasmus. "

"But I have no money," Erasmus protested.

"Neither did you when you got here. Tell the police you need to go back home, and you do not have any money, and I'm sure they will arrange a free trip for you" Casper suggested.

"Yeah man; Babylon always ready to do that," Fish agreed.

"Look here mate, since you got here what kind of job have you been doing?" Casper asked.

"All sort," Erasmus replied, horrified. "Construction site laborer, security man, street cleanser. I could have sold my blood for sixty quid a pint too only they wouldn't take mine."

All three collapsed into loud laughter.

"When I sick and in danger of dying, please nobody give me no poor man's blood," Fish jibed.

"You got yourself an easy life, mate," Casper said. "When I got here I sold stuff door to door. Now imagine a man who speaks no English come knocking at your door trying to sell you a telephone set. Lucky for me I eventually got this job with the council."

"I am not going to sweep no streets for nobody. I is a musician, man" Fish affirmed.

"From what I know there is no money in that either; it only keeps you on the benefits queue. But you can continue to receive unemployment benefits if you like; it doesn't go very far anymore, I'm sure. The way I see it, you should both be giving thanks instead of complaining. At least you always have the chance to get a decent meal to eat, and you are not in prison...yet," Casper teased. "

"Yeah man; London is full of good folks who become criminals without even trying, man. It's a tough city you know. Everywhere you see Babylon; going up and down, like madmen in Brixton," Fish agreed.

"Well, very soon I will be gone. I'm done with this place; I am praying that God will make a way for me to return home very soon. I think it is criminal to pay three hundred quid a month for a little room hardly big enough to take a small bed. Back home for that amount, I could rent a whole house," Erasmus sighed.

"God, I am starving," Fish said to himself. "Give me two pounds for a meal brother," he asked Casper.

"Why should I give you two pounds? And don't call me brother; we don't even look alike," Casper protested.

"Of course, we look alike bloodclat; are you color blind?" Fish scolded. "What about you Erasmus; I've got a great tip on a horse, and this is going to pay big money; lend me a fiver will you ?"

"You want to bet my hard-earned money on a horse; don't you have any shame? If you know what is good for you, get off your ass and go do some real work, understand? See you, idiots, later.

?" Erasmus sounded distressed. Finally deciding that he was in a hopelessly irredeemable company, he gathered his brush and picker and trundled off with his litter cart.

"Bloodclat," Fish summarized.

•   •   •   •   •

After the African guy had left Frank went to speak with Casper who had been left alone by himself. The West Indian guy had retired into studying the sports pages of a newspaper.

"Hi, I am Frank I called you yesterday, from Sam up in Eastham." Frank told Casper.

"Oh Frank, yes I do remember you. Heard Old Sam came to some grief."

"Yes he did; some people didn't fancy his style." Frank told him.

"I can understand that. So why are you here? What do you want to see me about?"

"Sam thought you could tell me a thing or two about some business called the Barefoot Revolution" Frank explained to him.

"Barefoot Revolution! Where you think you are, man? This is Brixton, not Zulu land." " Fish chuckled, roused from his reading.

"Shut up you?" Casper told him and led Frank away to another bench further away and at a spot which overlooked the huge Brixton Fridge building.

"So what do you want to know about the Barefoot Revolution?" Casper asked.

"Sam reasoned they may be behind some goings-on in the East End, some robberies and kidnappings and stuff," Frank lied to him.

Casper laughed, and then stopped to look at Frank as though he'd gone completely round the bend.

"No, you've got this all upside down, and I don't believe Sam could have said that. The Barefoot Revolution is not any kind of organization. It is just like, what do you call it, a philosophy. You don't go doing robberies, and kidnapping on the strength of a philosophy do you?"

Frank thought to mention Robin Hood but again thought not.

"You seem to know a lot about this don't you?" he pried further.

"Sure, I've got a few friends who are well into it. I mean in my time, You'll probably call them hippies. I met them while I was still working up there in Ilford, nice young fellows. Smoked a bit of pot they did otherwise completely harmless. Only I got a job here and we sort of lost regular contact."

"So you think I am on the wrong track then?" Frank was disappointed, but also very sure Casper was holding back much more than he was giving.

"Damn right, you are on the wrong track, and even on the wrong train sir," Casper affirmed.

It was a very disappointing conclusion to the chase.

• • • • •

A phone call came to Frank as he got off the train at Angel station; waiting for the bus back to Hackney.

"Hello is that Frank?" a hoarse female voice said.

"What if it is?" Frank wasn't in a good mood at all.

"Is that Frank?" She asked again like she hadn't heard the first time.

"Ok yes, this is Frank, who are you?"

"I have some news about your friend Sade," she said.

And Frank's heart sank.

CHAPTER 24

"I have some news about your friend Sade. We have your friend with us. She has not been harmed. But if you go to the police, this will be the last you will hear from us, and you will never see her again." the calm but raspy female voice said.

"Fuck! What do you want? Where are you?" Frank was agitated.

"Mind your language. I want you to follow my instructions completely. You will go to Liverpool Street station at six tomorrow evening and then wait there for the next instruction.," the voice instructed

"If you want me to bring some money I am sorry I don't have any to give you; but please don't hurt her," Frank pleaded. If they needed ransom money all he had in his bank account was about two thousand quid, and of course Sade's parents were far away in Africa.

"We will get to that later. And remember, she is safe yet. Any bad move from you and she will be history."

That but didn't sound nice at all to Frank, and he morosely nodded his head. He wasn't going to make any bad move.

"Toodle-doo," the woman said, and Frank thought he heard laughter in the background. His mind raced with alarm. What sort of criminal said things like "Toodle-doo," when they called you, but hopelessly psycho cases? Sade was certainly in serious danger.

●　　●　　●　　●　　●

There were very many questions: Who were these people? What were their intentions? How did he and Sade fit into this? What would become of them thereafter? Were they the same people who kidnapped Raj's daughter? That last one didn't quite fit yet. Rupinder was abducted for money. The people he was dealing with hadn't asked him for any money – not yet, however.

Nevertheless, he wondered why Liverpool Street had suddenly become the new hangout for body snatchers.

According to Casper, the Barefoot Revolution wasn't about this sort of thing. This probably meant that there was a more ruthless group to contend with. *She will be history*, the caller had said; that spoke of how dangerous they were. They were people who could kill to achieve their aims - whatever it was those aims were.

This presented him with another problem entirely. The next day was the Retro Renaissance gig with the Ex-Man. If things went wrong, he would not be able to make the gig. Trevor would be left hanging, and definitely, lose face, especially with his girlfriend who had done so much to arrange the gig. So Frank went to Trevor and explained everything as best as he could-

"I seem to have got myself and Sade in big trouble this time Trevor. I now realize I shouldn't have been messing with playing detective." He sighed.

"Keep calm; how did the caller sound? What is your impression of the caller's state of mind?" Trevor tried to assuage.

"Definitely insane. She said "Toodle-doo" before she switched off. Now, only psycho criminals talk that way, and this makes me even surer that Sade may be in great trouble." Frank despaired.

"According to you, they have made no demand yet?" Trevor asked

"None at all; and that is definitely perplexing. Raj's daughter was kidnapped for money, but these people have not asked me for any money. I am sure they know I have none, so what is the motive? Again, the ones who snatched Raj's daughter want the ransom delivered at Liverpool Street Station. Same place these other parties want me to go. Don't you see a connection, Trevor? Obviously, there is a ruthless and very dangerous network behind all this." Frank

"There are indeed many possibilities, but you need to keep calm. Do as they say and don't panic or attempt to make yourself a hero. You don't yet know the people you are dealing with." Trevor admonished.

"Exactly. Right now, I really can't presently think beyond the fact that I have risked the poor girl's life because of my foolishness. If anything happens to her, I am going to blame myself all of my life."

"Don't worry; nothing is going to happen to her; this is London. Tomorrow is the Ex-Man concert, Frank. I hope they set Sade free before the event." Trevor said.

"I'm sorry Trevor. That's me - one massive fuck up after another. But that is the situation right now. I might miss the gig. Why don't you bring in Heavy Dee as a backup? He's always been hanging around us for so long, asking to join up with us, and I am sure He's learned a bit."

"Oh no, not Heavy Dee; the audience will probably kill him. You know He's got no sense of rhythm," Trevor grimaced.

"You could go it alone Trevor. You're good, and nobody will miss me anyhow," Frank suggested. Trevor looked utterly downcast.

"I think I will have to ask the guys to get a replacement opening act. I know it will be short notice and they'd be pissed off. But I will make them know that it will be just an alternative arrangement. I am sure you will get his sorted out in good time."

"I'm really sorry Trevor. I didn't think this sort of shit could happen." Frank apologized.

"They want you to be at Liverpool Street Station tomorrow at five, right?"

"That's correct, but I get the feeling that I will be directed elsewhere from there, and they will only be using that place as a starting point to put a watch on me."

"You seem to have acquired some dangerous enemies lately. You say you have no idea who could be behind this?"

"Absolutely no idea."

"Anyhow, I will keep my fingers crossed that this will go well; and I guess all I can do is wish you luck." Trevor said.

●   ●   ●   ●   ●

Trevor came knocking on Frank's door later that night. With him was the Japanese kid Wu-Tan. He gave Frank a little black box half the size of a mobile phone.

"It is a screamer actually; one of the stuff Wu-Tan is also working on. Hit the little red dot, and you'll be surprised how much noise this little shit can make," Trevor told him. Frank said thanks; he wondered later how this screaming gadget could save his life or Sade's. But then in a desperate situation, any suggestion had great merits.

●   ●   ●   ●   ●

Moses Samuel stood in the middle of the first floor of Psychedelic Shack. , the huge the new fantasy store he had created, featuring a return to the 60s and 70s. Proudly, he admired the displays. Most of the items were Chinese- made replicas, so carefully crafted to his instructions that they could well have passed for originals. There were grandfather clocks, jukeboxes, radiograms, transistor radios, Polaroid cameras and thousands of other memorabilia. Moses Samuel's favorites were two sections. One was the music bay for which he had bought thousands of wax records from vintage record shops in the USA. It featured a massive rock selection and an even bigger blues and soul catalog. The music bay stocked no CDs, only records, tapes and 8-tracks, since CDs were unknown in the seventies. His other favorite section and the one which excited him the most was the African bay in the middle of which he had mounted a life-size statue of a Masai warrior in battle leap, complete with shield and fighting club. He, of course, knew that not all Africans are Masai, but that didn't matter to Moses Samuel; He just loved the statue.

Around him also stood Sasha, Nancy, Sade and several other merchandisers with goods on display on the shelves and other places around the huge store.

"We open tomorrow. How are the opening arrangements getting along?" he asked Sasha.

"Well, as you instructed we are not having any newspaper and television promotion yet, we are doing the minimum of the traditional stuff, so I guess we are pretty well covered. The main event comes up later in the day. I think that is pretty well covered also."

"Absolutely; we can't afford to have a sell-out in a single day, can we? Also mustn't lose sight of the objective of this all – which is to bring people to the awareness. We do have the website set up though?"

"No problem at all. It is at psychedelic-shack dot co dot uk "

"Perfect. Online orders can be delayed. It is the walk-in purchases we need to worry about. How are the footprint crews going?"

"They are getting ready to go. Before dawn tomorrow, they will be on the move. Casper is in charge, and He's assured that there won't be any hitch. Someone called Erasmus would be laying the decals from Brixton Station. Freaky guy, Casper says He's doing this in exchange for a ticket back to Africa. Another whose name is Fish will be laying footprints from Elephant and Castle. The tough bit is the route from Clapham Junction, but Casper says He's got six persons working on it all night," Sasha told Moses Samuel.

"Perfect; it would be fun to see people follow those footsteps just to see where they lead," he laughed.

• • • • •

Next morning Raj got another phone call. "You will take the briefcase of money and go to Liverpool Street Station today at exactly four forty-five."

"Liverpool Street Station?" Raj asked, very confused indeed.

"You know where that is, don't you?"

"Yes, Liverpool Street Station, I know" Raj told the caller.

"There is a coffee shop near the entrance. You will buy a cup of hot chocolate."

"Yes I know the shop; a cup of hot chocolate costs three pounds at the shop" Raj complained.

"Shut up will you and listen to me," the caller reprimanded." You will buy a cup of hot chocolate. You will sit down and drink it; shouldn't take more than ten minutes. Then you will leave without the briefcase of money."

"Where will I find my daughter after?" Raj was more interested to know.

"You will not find her; she will come home tonight by herself."

"Why should I believe you?" Raj certainly was not prepared to be taken for a fool. What if that silly detective had been right, and the money and his daughter vanished forever?

"Because you have no choice," said the voice, hanging up.

Raj stared at the phone for a while; irritated. Then he called Frank's phone. Getting no response, he called Kalyan.

"Kalyan, will you please come right away," he told his future son-in-law.

• • • • •

When Frank left home at five for the rendezvous, he had no idea that he was being followed. Bill Mulligan, Andy Wagstaff, and Michael Barlow, and of course Harvey Simpson had been hanging around his house most of the afternoon with a diabolic plan in hatching. Their initial plan had been to abduct Frank, take him away in their van to a safe place and torture the truth out of him about where Ida was hiding. The plan was scuttled by the police patrol car which had unreasonably chosen to stop on the road nearby when Frank finally emerged from the house.

"That was lucky. We could all have spent years in the slammer for that." Andy Wagstaff wheezed,

"Never mind, let's just follow him to where he is going until we get another opportunity to grab him. Michael Barlow was more optimistic.

The three could do no more than watch helplessly as their quarry went off to board a bus, which they faithfully followed.

•   •   •   •   •

Raj got to the station at five forty-five as instructed. Grudgingly, he bought a hot chocolate; complained about how bad it tasted and then went to sit on the bench the caller told him to use - the one furthermost from foot traffic. Across the road waited Kalyan as Raj had instructed, faithfully keeping a watch. Raj finished his hot chocolate, pushed the briefcase under the bench as instructed and angrily chucked the cup in a waste bin before leaving. He did not, however, return home as instructed. He walked right through the huge Liverpool Street station building, exited on the far side, turned to the left and then walked back alongside the building and across the road to join Kalyan. Together, they went into a nearby supermarket and from within waited and watched the coffee shop in front of the station.

•   •   •   •   •

Frank got to the station with five minutes to spare, but was pleased nevertheless that he wasn't late. The phone call came at exactly six.

"Are you there now?" the caller asked.

"Yes I am"

"Okay, go to the coffee shop in front; buy a cup of hot chocolate and go sit at the furthermost bench on the left, under which you will find a briefcase. You will sit on this bench, finish your hot chocolate, then you will get on the bus going to Clapham Junction."

"Why not the train to Clapham Junction?" Frank asked needlessly.

"Just do as you have been told," the caller rebuked, abruptly hanging up.

Frank did as instructed, bought himself a hot chocolate, found the briefcase, picked it up and went for the bus queue.

"Oi, that's not yours, you bleeding thief!" the florist nearby chided, but Frank ignored the florist, who returned to his stand muttering and lamenting how nobody's property was safe anymore

From across the street, Raj and Kalyan watched, stunned.

"Something told me that man is not a detective. A crook I can tell from a mile away. Bloody robber, he is the kidnapper. No wonder he refused to bring the money. It is because he is the kidnapper." Raj fumed. "

And as Frank entered the bus headed for Clapham Junction, Kalyan and Raj hailed a taxi. "Follow that bus," Kalyan told the taxi.

•　　•　　•　　•　　•

Harvey and his crew had put a "Men at Work" sign around their van to enable them to wait without harassment. They too quickly picked up their stuff and followed the bus.

Trevor had also arrived early and had been watching Frank from a KFC which was about a hundred yards away. Unlike the others, he wasn't in any hurry. He had this morning reminded Frank not to forget the panic device and was pleased that Frank had remembered. Not that it was any kind of alarm equipment. Beside him, Wu-Tan opened up a device which looked like a small tablet computer and switched it on. A road map of London came up on the screen. Wu-Tan zoomed in to get a distinct map which showed where they were sitting and a few miles further south. Having done this, he slotted another device which looked like a USB drive into the side of the computer. A flashing red dot came up on the map, slowly advancing along with Frank's bus. Wu-Tan handed Trevor the small computer, gave a thumb up, and left.

CHAPTER 25

"You will get off at Camberwell Green," another phone call instructed Frank while he was on the bus.

The mystery behind the hooligans who had chased him on his street, days ago had finally come to light, the previous evening. Instead of the greased paper the stalker had this night left the copy of a parking ticket at his door. On the back of the paper was the same illiterate scrawl:

"*I no were u live ediot.*"

Frank remembered the burly bricklayer that he had given a parking ticket; the bricklayer with serpents tattooed all over his arms and murder in his eyes. But Frank wasn't afraid anymore; there were far more important things to worry about. If he survived the current day it would merely be a matter of making a complaint to the police, and the fool's goose would be cooked.

At this point though, all that occupied his mind even more than the thought of seeing Sade free again was how to escape going to prison. Along the way he had peeked inside the briefcase, having persuaded himself that it wasn't an explosive device. It was not locked, and Frank found himself looking at stacks of currency bills.

"What the fuck," he said to himself as he quickly shut the briefcase again, looking carefully all around to make sure nobody had been watching. He took another look. Yes, it was money; a lot of it. He also found a little pink envelope on top of the stack. Frank took out the envelope and then shut the briefcase.

The envelope was addressed to "*Rupinder,*" and inside was a little card with lots of pink hearts printed on it. He read:

"*I love you Rupie*" xxxx Kalyan"

The realization of what was happening hit him like a huge fist in the chest. He was being used to deliver the ransom money after all.

How Raj had been able to put this together thoroughly baffled him. Otherwise, if it hadn't been Raj's doing and if the police were already on this case that meant he was being watched; and if he was being watched, that meant he was a candidate for being mistaken for the kidnapper. One option that occurred to him was to leave the briefcase of money in the bus and run. He decided instead to play along. Eventually, he should find the kidnappers and when he did, so will the police if they were tailing. After the arrests had been made, he could take his chance at proving innocence.

He disembarked at Camberwell Green, crossed the road and walked up the next street as instructed. There seemed to be some unusual activity ahead as he could see. A scattering of strangely-dressed person walked past him, most of them carried fluorescent rainbow-color shopping bags with a large logo which read "Psychedelic Shack." Most were dressed like hippies, straight out of the sixties: flower print tops, headbands, choker necklaces and all. A couple went past him barefoot. The woman gave him a V-sign with her left hand. "Peace," she said, with a goofy smile. Yes, something very unusual was definitely happening ahead.

As instructed, Frank followed a trail of black footprint decals laid on the sidewalk about three feet apart, and soon saw that they led to a gigantic crowded shopping store, with buntings and huge banners which read "Grand Opening.." From the façade hanged a thirty-foot wide sign which said, "Psychedelic Shack."

The huge car park in the front was crowded, not only with cars but also more of the characters like he had met while on his way here. It looked like he had strayed into a warp with the sixties. Many wore rubber sandals hacked out of car tires, many more were without shoes. Frank could see no police car around and would think this unusual as a traffic problem seemed imminent. He found the reason in a moment though – a pocket of young people were gathered near the entrance carrying provocative placards one of which was a picture of a pig wearing a police cap. Thus it made sense that any police here would be in mufti.

Not quite sure of what to do next, Frank mingled with the crowd and went inside Psychedelic Shack. The hall had been gaudily done up in rainbow colors. The shelves were stacked with stuff from another generation. A dazzling display carried intricately carved jukeboxes, standing television, standing radios with record changers, gramophones with fluted horn speakers. It was like stepping at least fifty years back in time. Frank also was drawn to a display which he thought Sade would probably have loved. It had been set up behind a Zulu warrior. The display was filled with colorful African dresses and seeing them made his heartache. It reminded him of Sade.

His phone rang. "Where are you?" The now familiar voice of the caller came to him.

"Inside the fucking store," Frank by now had lost all desire to remain civil.

"Yeah I know, but where exactly?" she asked.

"How the hell am I supposed to know, it's a fucking jungle in here isn't it?" he rasped.

The caller giggled. "*Okee dokee*; never mind, just walk to the back of the store, and there you will see a sign pointing to the basement. It says "BASEMENT" Take the stairs down." Off went the phone once more.

Frank thought this was getting very irritating. Frank followed the instructions nevertheless, walking right through the hundred-foot deep store toward the back. Along the way, he thought he saw someone who looked like Ida. The lady he saw was a long way away though, and their eyes had met for only a brief second before she vanished again into the aisles.

Frank took the steps, down to the basement and was at the bottom met by a plump lady wearing a black dress, plenty of beads and a John Lennon type glasses.

"Helloooo!" She sang; offering her hand.

"Who the fuck are you?" Frank wasn't amused. He had resolved to go down with all dignity if that was what would be finally demanded of him.

"My name is Sasha," the lady said. But Frank had lost interest in Sasha. He stood gaping at the other delicately dressed up woman standing nearby smiling.

"Hi Frank," Nancy said to him.

"What the fuck is going on here? "Frank said to her.

●   ●   ●   ●   ●

Back in the car park, Harvey Simpson and his crew parked the van and waited to discuss what to do next. Things were not going anywhere like what they planned at all.

"Looks like fun in there. Fuck me, I say why are we sitting outside here; lets go see what's happening," Bill Mulligan finally suggested. And so they had abandoned their watch from the car park and gone into the store. Once inside they'd all quickly become transformed into greedy kids, and in fifteen minutes were wheeling around trolleys piled with vintage ware - clocks, mugs, lamps, phones, records, caps, t-shirts, jeans, and other stuff.

Harvey Simpson, on a lone adventure away from the others, was standing in the middle of an aisle admiring a star-studded black leather jacket and thinking how different he would look in it. Oh, wouldn't all the young chicks just die when they saw him in this, and Ida could very well be gone for good for all he cared.

"Excuse me," the familiar voice of the lady trying to squeeze by came to him. Time and motion froze. Harvey turned, Ida turned in her step. Both found themselves looking straight into the eyes of one another. Harvey screamed in surprise. Ida screamed in terror.

CHAPTER 26

Frank was in for more surprises as he followed Sasha and Nancy into a hall in the basement of Psychedelic Shack. The small hall was as gaudily furnished as the store upstairs. Sitting behind a huge table at the furthermost end was a white guy, head shaved clean. He wore a colorful dashiki – which looked quite alien to his very English looks. He also wore dark aviator sunglasses. Behind him, and scattered around the hall were several African carvings. Behind him also stood Casper who winked at Frank and gave him an amused smile.

It got more bizarre as he looked. Scattered around the hall were several pod chairs and on one of them sat Rupinder. She didn't look anyhow like Rupinder though. Gone were the sari and the golden ornaments. She now wore a bright flowered long-sleeved blouse on faded bell-bottom blue jeans and about a ton of beads around the neck. Her unhidden disdain for Frank remained nevertheless. She stood from the seat, walked gracefully up to Frank and took the briefcase from him.

"This is for me. I suppose," she said.

Stunned into submission, Frank further looked around the room to discover Fernandez from the East End Mirror, and Abu, the Pakistani he had given over to the police at Tower Hill. Around Abu"s neck hung the object of Frank's most fervent pursuit. Abu was wearing The Crooked Bullet. And as Frank's eyes locked upon the lucky charm, his fears and bewilderment were momentarily replaced by the thought of the ten thousand pounds prize that was now almost within grasp.

"Now what the heck is happening here?" he hoarsely asked no one in particular.

The hairless hunk behind the desk took off his sunglasses and folded it on the desk before him.

"Well, well; finally face to face with the detective. You nearly gave us a scare too you know."

"How do you mean? Frank asked.

"My name is Moses Samuel; but friends call me Rabbi Zulu," the man said.

Despite the perceived danger, Frank almost laughed. Rabbi Zulu. This certainly was beginning to look like a loony bin.

"No worries," Moses Samuel apparently understood. He looked in Fernandez's direction, and as if that was a cue, Fernandez came over to Frank and gave him a sheaf of printed paper. Frank recognized that they had been printed from his stolen computer. They contained the draft of his *East End Heists* story.

"How did you get this?" he needlessly asked:

"Never mind where or how" Moses Samuel told him. "More important is that it is full of false assumptions and I must say a poorly constructed story.

"So what is the truth, and who made you experts on writing stories; never mind that you guys need to do some explanation about my computer?" Frank found himself getting angry.

""You robbed my flat? You little shit. You should end up in prison for that." Frank turned upon Fernandez.

●　　　●　　　●　　　●　　　●

Moses Samuel reached behind him, brought Frank's computer and slid it across the table. "That's your computer; you can't be doing so well if you can't afford something better than this," he said. Frank made no move to get his computer.

Moses Samuel continued: "Now as I was saying, the story made a very lazy conclusion about, robberies, kidnappings, and of course the Barefoot Revolution, which is purely a figment of someone's imagination. It is a completely silly story not that it wouldn't have The Times hiring you if you could prove the story, but then there is really no hope of that happening because there is no story. "

"I beg your pardon. There were robberies; I witnessed one. They were kidnapping, my girlfriend and this young lady here were abducted. And yes, a friend did tell me that some asshole group called Barefoot Revolution could be involved." Frank insisted. "

"You mean the drama at the bank in Hackney? That is where you could have got me severely embarrassed. You see, that bank was indeed robbed. Why was it robbed? Friends of mine lost their money to the bank, and I simply wanted to discomfit the bank. Actually, I returned the money later because I had a rethink; so there really was no money stolen. And of course the other robbery you wrote about never happened," Moses Samuel said.

"You stole that lucky charm, and then you kidnapped this woman here," Frank pointed first at Abu and then at Rupinder.

Moses Samuel laughed. "You've got such a fantastic imagination. When I worked as a crime reporter, I used mine more wisely. Are you by familiar with the name Phil Jenner?"

Frank now remembered why he thought the guy looked familiar.

"You are Phil Jenner?"

"The one and only" Moses Samuel nodded.

"I can't believe this. You were my grief for many years. My boss at the East End Mirror never imagined I could ever do anything well enough because of you. I'd been for years wondering where you disappeared to since you left The Independent" Frank couldn't hold back his excitement.

"You mean Spencer Cowley? He's retired now, with a lot of money in the bank," Moses Samuel told him.

"What do you mean? East End Mirror will never make enough money for Spencer to retire on," Frank was puzzled.

"He got lucky. I bought his newspaper. David here now runs East End Mirror." Moses Samuel told him. David Fernandez beamed proudly.

"So what do you plan to do with me?" Frank had no idea what to think anymore.

"We'll come to that in a moment. First a little bit of education. Do you know that animals have souls?" Moses Samuel asked.

"I don't know what that means, and I really may not care," Frank truthfully replied.

"What it means is that they have emotions and memories like human beings, and the only thing that makes them different is that we kill them just because we believe, they have no feelings. We can kill them anyhow and to us, anyhow is okay? Just imagine someone picking you off the street slitting your throat and making shoes and handbags out of your skin."

"Of course, that is never going to happen, there are laws against that sort of behavior; Frank said uneasily.

"Absolutely, the problem is that the law has been made by human beings for human beings, and a different set of laws exist for other non-human beings, and it says they have no rights"

"So you are for animal rights then, I suppose?"

"More than that. The Barefoot Revolution, as you call it, believes in back to nature as a style of living clothes, food, and habits that are as near nature as possible. So, to us not wearing shoes is more than a mere protest against the use of animal as items of clothing, but it is a gesture which has deeper significance and seeks to emphasize a respect for nature."

"Apparently, your intention is to get everyone walking barefoot. That, is the kookiest notion I've ever heard. It will never happen," Frank honestly told him.

"Maybe; but think about it. If we can convince Britain to do this, how great an echo it will make all over the world. Think of the effect this will have on the decline of crime and corruption. Why steal when you've found that you can actually do without the stuff you would buy with the money."

"Of course, this is unlikely to happen, not in a million years. What have you guys been smoking? Must be something very scary." Frank insisted.

"You don't have to agree with me; not that it matters if you do in any case. But we will get there eventually; we will win England one man, one woman, one child at a time," Moses Samuel dismissed him with a wave of his hand.

"So how are you going to do that; the way I see this You'll be in prison very soon; the whole lot of you"", Frank told him.

"And how is this going to happen unless you go saying things that you have no business saying, to people who have no business learning about them?"

"I see you've got my notes and computer, but never mind I can rewrite them anyway. I have them all in my head here," Frank tapped his head.

"I don't see anyone taking you very seriously. Fernandez here could write rings around you, and I've kept him close to me for several years. And as a matter of fact, next week, he is going to publish his own version of what you called The East End Robberies, completely repudiating everything that you have gathered together, so much that any other newspaper would think you are completely nuts when you send in your version. In any case, I want you, as a matter of fact, to give me a reason why we should let you leave this place alive." Moses Samuel told him

"Because a lot of people saw me come here," Frank became unnerved.

"I wish I could take that as a reason. As a matter of fact, you could be easily disappeared, and Fernandez here could cook up a beautiful story about whatever misfortune which might have mysteriously befallen you."

"You don't mean you're really going to kill me?" Frank dismayed.

"There is a good possibility that might happen, the way this is playing out."

"Where is my girlfriend?" Frank licked dry lips, with a dry tongue.

"How romantic." Moses Samuel laughed. "Even when faced with your own terminal misfortune you can still remain worried about your girlfriend. We should return then to the subject of abductions. What do you have to say, Rupinder?"

"The lucky charm was not stolen; I took it." Rupinder said, defiant and contemptuous. "And as you can see Mister Detective, I have not been kidnapped; I needed the money to escape away from my father."

She sharply caught her voice and nearly fell over from her seat as two men stumbled dazed into the room. They were Raj and Kalyan. They both stood for a long while, staring at Rupinder.

"What have you done to my daughter you silly creature?" Raj asked Frank. Frank shrugged his shoulders.

"Nothing that she didn't need to get done to her. We uncovered the woman beneath all that shell of boredom, and we changed her to a woman who is alive," Moses Samuel said.

"I didn't want her to be alive this way; I want her to be my daughter. Rupinder take off that silly get-up at once and come with me," Raj agonized.

"You mean take them off right here Papa?" Rupinder asked.

"No, no not here. Go away and fetch your clothes and then come with me."

"But I don't want my clothes, I want these ones. I am not a child," obstinately.

"A headache you are giving me, my dear. What have these animals done to you? First, they kidnap you and ask for money, and then your mind they kidnap" Raj held his head as if in pain.

"I was not kidnapped Papa; I came to them by myself," petulantly.

"Is that so? Then why did they ask me for two hundred thousand pounds ransom money?"

"They did not ask for the money, I did. I wanted to escape away to Europe. Papa, you are killing me with too much care."

"So you betray your poor father so that you can walk barefoot all over England like this, and smoke poisonous weeds? "Raj looked about to cry.

"Come with me, Rupie," Kalyan spoke for the first time; on his knees before Rupinder. But Raj was no more interested in this. His eyes were fixed on Abu and on the missing lucky charm around his neck. Raj made a sudden dash to retrieve it, but Abu was nimbler than he looked; jumping quickly to the side, as Raj came crashing to the floor.

"Give that to me you thief!" Raj shouted.

"If you take that thing, Papa, I will not go ahead with the marriage" Rupinder warned Raj.

"Why not? It is our lucky charm," Kalyan was puzzled.

"Oh no, it is not our lucky charm, it is a cursed thing "Rupinder grieved.

"Why do you say that Rupie? It cannot be a cursed thing to have a lucky charm," Kalyan more puzzled.

"Ask Papa, but I am sure he will not tell you. But I will tell you anyway for your own good. It is said that anyone who takes possession of that charm will have a bent penis. I don't want my husband to have a bent penis."

Very much unnerved, Abu carefully took the charm off his neck and placed it firmly in Raj's hand. Having done this, he dashed for the toilet, apparently to thoroughly examine himself for damage.

"Come with me Rupie I promise to make you happy," Kalyan resumed his pleading. Rupinder shook her head firmly.

"I can't Kalyan, you are boring. I want to feel alive" Rupinder shook her head.

"Boring?" Kalyan was miffed. "Wait a minute," he said, dashing out of the room and pounding up the stairs.

•   •   •   •   •

Up in the store, Ida's scream brought her boyfriend Jimmy running. His protest was cut very short as Bill Mulligan clobbered him unconscious, with a Mickey Mouse painted skittle. And as Jimmy collapsed on the floor, Ida's scream of fear turned into a mad growl.

"What did you do that for you mad brutes," she launched herself at Bill Mulligan who promptly clobbered her too, dropping her unconscious on top of her boyfriend. Without much care, Bill Mulligan picked Ida up, slung her limp body over his shoulder, and casually announced to the rest:

"Let's go, we've got her now. "

But Harvey Simpson only starred dumbfounded at Mulligan.

"You have just destroyed my life you buffoon," he wailed in distress; calculating how many years they would all likely spend in prison as a result of this misadventure.

•   •   •   •   •

When Kalyan returned to the basement a few minutes later, he was carrying a boom box which he had borrowed from a shelf upstairs. He also had a cassette tape in his hand. He placed the boom box on the floor, pushed the cassette tape into the machine, hit the play button and cranked up the volume.

A soulful Indian song rumbled out of the loudspeaker, which Kalyan proceeded to accompany with a serenade. Rupinder recognized the tune from the film Love in Tokyo, once her mother's favorite.

le gayi dil gudiya jaapaan ki
le gayi dil gudiya jaapaan ki
paagal mujhe kar diya
paagal mujhe kar diya
jaapaan
love in tokyo

Kalyan was now doing a dazzling ballet dance which had Rupinder staring spellbound. She fell breathless into Kalyan's arms as the song concluded.

Rupinder picked up the briefcase of cash and placed it on the table before Moses Samuel.

"Please keep this as my contribution to the cause," she tearfully said; then allowed herself to be led away by her husband to be and her father.

"Well, well, another satisfied customer," Moses Samuel applauded. "But she will be back I promise you, and next time she will bring her husband along with her. So what will it be Frank Wire, detective extraordinaire; how would you prefer this to go? "

"I still think it sucks big time," Frank told him, his confidence renewed.

"No you suck big time" Moses Samuel said, and Frank suddenly found himself staring into the enormous muzzle of a pistol.

"Take off your shoes Frankie or I will blow your head off. I will count to five. One...two...three...four..."

Desperately Frank attempted to yank his shoes off.

"Too late…" Moses Samuel viciously announced. Frank shut his eyes expecting to feel a bullet smashing into his skull. There was indeed a loud clap of metal against metal and then silence. Frank smiled thinking dying wasn't so bad after all. Then he heard her laugh. Frank opened his eyes to find Sade standing in front of him. She took his face in her hands.

"Oh you poor boy, you went through all this just for me "she hugged him and kissed him.

"Don't tell me you are in this too," Frank was flustered.

Sade nodded." And I am so proud of you Frank; that you could do this for me."

But Frank was not in the least amused.

"I guess I might have been wrong about you then. Here you were camped up with a bunch of lunatics while I am getting frantic and risking my life for nothing" he sadly shook his head.

"Bunch of lunatics? Frank, you ought to see the magnificent display they gave me up there in the store," Sade didn't agree.

"Don't tell me you will be walking all over without shoes too. I am thoroughly disappointed about all this Sade. I just feel like I don't know you anymore."

Frank walked to the table, picked up his computer and turned to go. He stopped for a brief moment to look Sade in the face. He imagined that he could very clearly see in it that "glowing" which Maureen had warned him about. The glowing that told you your woman was cheating on you.

"Frank, I am sorry; it was just a joke," Sade pleaded.

Frank found his way blocked by Nancy and Sasha.

"You were doing great Frank. You risked everything for love, and that is so absolutely romantic. Don't return to being an asshole," Nancy said to him.

"As a matter of fact, we put her up to this. It wasn't her idea at all. We really gave her no choice," Sasha added. And when Frank looked back to Sade, he saw tears rolling down her cheeks, her eyes pleading. Nevertheless, for him, self-respect remained paramount.

"You guys really have to move aside now; I've got a show to catch. We will talk about this later," he said to them.

"So have I," said a voice from the door. It was Trevor. Frank was astounded.

"Hey, what are you doing here Trevor; how did you find me?"

Trevor showed him his small computer. He tapped the screen with a finger, and the device on Frank's belt beeped, a little red light flashing from its side.

"I tracked your movement from the train station. But when you got off at Camberwell Green, it was no more necessary. I knew where to find you from there," Trevor said to him.

Behind Trevor where three heavies, wearing black Ex-Man concert vests.

"You knew how to find me from there; how?" Frank was a lot more confused. Moses Samuel laughed from behind him.

"The Ex-Man knows everything," Moses Samuel said to him. Frank looked at Moses Samuel, at Trevor and back to Moses Samuel.

"You are the Ex-Man?" Frank could barely talk. All around, the entire room had gone very quiet; and no one was smiling. As the new realization sunk in, he thought to say something to Trevor, but still, no word came. Trevor nodded.

"Let's go Frank, you've got a concert to open," Trevor said to him.

Moses Samuel attempted to explain a bit further. "You see, we found real talent in need of a hand up, and we gave it to him. Not only that, we created a superstar. The concert is going to make Ex-Man stronger still. But, and nobody knows this yet, we have actually organized the concert to promote our cause as well as this exotic shopping experience that we have created here in Psychedelic Shack. By the end of this night, the entire world will know about Psychedelic Shack, and by their end of this night, at least half of the audience in that concert will go home without their shoes, all ambassadors for the cause. The same we did to your girlfriend too. We found real talent in need of a hand up, and we gave it to her. Do I still look a lunatic, Frank?"

"We'd better go now, or we are going to be late. The opening acts have already begun," Trevor emphasized the urgency.

• • • • •

"Nowhere are you going all of you," Raj angrily cried as he burst into the room, followed by four police. "Arrest them, officers. Arrest them for robbery and kidnapping and stealing my money," Raj raved.

He hunted all over the room for the briefcase and having found it, hoisted it up triumphantly as evidence. "You will be going to the prison, all of you," he promised.

CHAPTER 27

All hopes seemed lost. The concert was at this rate going to become a failure, Frank despaired

"This is the Ex-Man, He's got a concert to get to immediately," Frank told the police.

"I don't care if He's Spider Man. You'll all have to go down to the station," a policeman said; while another read them their rights and yet another called on the phone for a wagon. At this moment Fernandez who had been silently watching for so long stepped forward, holding an object in each raised hand. They were grenades. As he came to the middle of the room and toward the police, he pulled the safety pins out of the grenades with his teeth.

"Let them go, or we are all going to die, and I am not joking," Fernandez threatened.

The police drew back in fear; Raj dived to the floor in panic.

"There is no escape. You can't get out of this, more officers will be outside waiting for you," a more courageous policeman warned.

Moses Samuel seemed to be considering the situation with more casualness than required. Finally, he stood, pressed a button on the wall behind him and a panel slid open, to reveal a garage, inside which was a Toyota van. Casper got the driver's door of the van open and started the engine.

Moses Samuel looked at Trevor, Frank, and everyone in the room and said: "We've got a show to catch."

And while Fernandez covered the police with his primed grenade, everyone else dashed for the bus, which was soon racing away through the back alley, and away from Psychedelic Shack.

Several minutes after they were gone, Fernandez to the utmost alarm of the police and to Raj's screaming terror, dropped one of the grenades on the floor. Then, very calmly, he flipped open the top of the other to reveal a propane lighter with which he lit a cigarette.

"You can get one of these lighters for nineteen ninety-nine upstairs in the store," he told them. "Cool, isn't it?"

And they all fell upon Fernandez and beat him to a pulp.

●　　●　　●　　●　　●

The Ex-Man concert rocked the whole of Britain. Millions watched it on television. Five thousand watched it from the 02 venue, outside of which were fifty police, waiting to effect arrests when the show ended.

EPILOGUE

Moses Samuel was acquitted of all criminal charges. The Barefoot Revolution became a huge force all over the world with Woodstock as the new Mecca and Rabbi Zulu the new spiritual leader. Finally, he sold off Woodstock and Psychedelic Shack in a tough bidding war between Amazon.com and Google and bought an island off the Congo, where nobody is permitted to wear shoes.

Frank O'Dwyer became manager to his friend Trevor Cook, the Ex-Man. He soon kicked the job and bought a nightclub in Brixton. He also continued to work as a private investigator

Trevor Cook kicked his job at Newham Council and became a pop star. His label *Def Adam* signed on several old-time pop music icons to rock the world once again.

Sade's success exploded enormously and with money from Moses Samuel she started her own clothing line *Sweet Taboo* which became very popular worldwide.

Abu Bhutto became the owner of a successful investigating business after listening to the CDs he had nicked from Frank's flat. He spends his leisure time clandestinely watching dodgy pizza and kebab shops and recommending them for closure.

Sasha Cohen was retained by Google to run Psychedelic Shack and Woodstock. She married Nancy Hughes.

Ida Simpson filed an assault charge against Harvey and his gang. She was persuaded by the gang to drop the charges. She filed for divorce nevertheless and escaped away to the USA with Jimmy.

Harvey Simpson suffered a breakdown. His business ruined by the divorce and drink, he could be seen wandering all over London piss drunk.

Rupinder and Kalyan got married, returned to India to start a film producing business. They became well known for making big hit Indian musical love films.

Sam Donahue decided to go straight. He lost all his money to Internet fraudsters and suffered a stroke. He was mugged and killed on his way back home one night in his electric wheelchair.

Spencer Cowley became a born again Christian and went off to live as a missionary in Haiti with his wife.

David Fernandez became the new owner of East End Mirror.
Raj sold Bhatti's Jewelries and bought a traveling circus where he had his own magic shows – hypnotizing the audience. Nobody knows yet what he did with The Crooked Bullet.

NOTE FROM THE AUTHOR

Word-of-mouth is crucial for any author to succeed. If you enjoyed the book, please leave a review online—anywhere you are able. Even if it's just a sentence or two. It would make all the difference and would be very much appreciated.

Thanks!
Rotimi

About the Author

Rotimi Ogunjobi is a satirist, playwriter, novelist and filmmaker. Some of his writings have been published in several countries of the world. His short stories have won local awards, and one of his novels has been on the long list for an international award.

Thank you so much for reading one of our **Crime Fiction** novels.
If you enjoyed the experience, please check out our recommended
title for your next great read!

Caught in a Web by Joseph Lewis

"This important, nail-biting crime thriller about MS-13 sets the
bar very high. One of the year's best thrillers."
–BEST THRILLERS

CPSIA information can be obtained
at www.ICGtesting.com
Printed in the USA
LVHW111053080719
623426LV00001B/122/P